OUTSIDE SHOOTER

The buzzer sounded, and Deke stepped forward at the sideline to greet his players coming off the court for the last moment before the start of the game.

The roar of the crowd rolled down out of the bleachers all around him. The combo still was blaring away from its position out of sight under the bleachers. The cheerleaders were skipping at the center of the court, clapping their hands in time to the music. The lights seemed brighter than ever.

Deke dropped to one knee and leaned into the group of players around him—the five starters standing in front, and the substitutes behind them.

In the center of the group six pairs of hands—Deke's and the starters'—gripped, pumped once, and released.

"Go get 'em," Deke said, and he stepped back to watch his first basketball team take the court for the first time.

Also by Thomas J. Dygard

Backfield Package
Forward Pass
Game Plan
Halfback Tough
Infield Hit
Outside Shooter
Quarterback Walk-on
Rebound Caper
The Rebounder
River Danger
The Rookie Arrives
Running Wild
Second Stringer
Tournament Upstart
Wilderness Peril

Thomas J. Dygard

OUTSIDE SHOOTER

William Morrow and Company New York 1979

BEECH TREE
New York

Published by Morrow Junior Books
a division of William Morrow and Company, Inc.
1350 Avenue of the Americas, New York, NY 10019
www.williammorrow.com

Printed in the United States of America.

The Library of Congress has cataloged the Morrow Junior Books edition of *Outside Shooter* as follows:
Dygard, Thomas J.
Outside shooter.
Summary: A high school basketball star's personality problems threaten not only his own career but the success of the whole team.
ISBN 0-688-22177-7 (trade)—ISBN 0-688-32177-1 (library)
[1. Basketball—Fiction] I. Title. PZ7.D98930u [Fic] 78-24002

First Beech Tree Edition, 1998
ISBN 0-688-16367-X
10 9 8 7 6 5 4 3 2 1

Deke Warden heard about Bobby Haggard the first day he set foot in Bloomfield to take up residence as basketball coach of the Bulldogs.

It was the week before Labor Day—a bright, warm afternoon with the first slight hints of autumn in the air. Unmistakably, summer was ending and another school year was about to begin.

The Bloomfield High football team was already at work, nearing the end of the first full week of practice. Deke had seen them on the drill field when he drove past the school.

The start of basketball practice was six weeks away.

Turning a corner just three blocks from the school, Deke pulled to the curb in front of a row of two-story red-brick apartments. He stepped out of the car and began carrying bundles inside.

With his short-cropped blond hair and a clear face dotted with a dozen freckles, Deke Warden looked hardly older than the boys he was going to be coaching. He was tall, standing six feet, seven inches, and he was brawny, carrying a muscular 230 pounds packed onto his frame. In his jeans, T-shirt, and sneakers without socks, he looked less like a high-school basketball coach than the college player he had been last year—a second-team All-American selection on a winning team at Illinois State University.

But Deke's playing days were over, and he was the new coach of the Bloomfield High Bulldogs, one of the leading teams in the high-school-basketball hotbed of western Illinois.

The thought thrilled Deke. It was what he had always wanted: his own high-school basketball team, to coach, to teach, to shape, to direct.

As a college player, Deke had all of the ingredients—size, speed, and shooting ability—to attract the professional teams. And they came after him. They chased him all through his senior year. They dangled glittering contract offers for a professional career. They were certain that he was precisely what they wanted for their free-swinging, wild-shooting style of play. He was going to be a star. They all told him so.

From the start Deke gave them the same answer. He was hanging up his uniform and ending his playing days when he graduated from Illinois State. He was through playing. He wanted to be a high-school coach. He had never wanted to be anything else. The time had come. He was ready now, and he was going to do it. He did not want to play professional basketball. That was not in his plans. He was not going to change his mind.

All the same, the Philadelphia 76ers drafted Deke in the first round of the National Basketball Association drawings.

Then they found that Deke Warden meant what he said. True, he did not yet have a job on that day back in the early spring. But he was going to be a high-school basketball coach—and that was that.

Even now Deke was more than a little amazed to find himself moving into an apartment in Bloomfield, moving into the coaching job at Bloomfield High. He was fortunate to be stepping straight into one of the top high-school coaching jobs in this part of the state.

On the record, Deke Warden was untried as a coach. True, he had studied hard with the idea of becoming one. As a player, he had tried to point every move toward being a coach one day. He observed his own coaches closely. He noted their every success and failure. In his mind he measured their techniques—in handling players, in devising strategy, in conducting drills. Along the way, he coached whenever the opportunity presented itself. He had directed church-league teams and fraternity teams all through college. But still, when it came to a job record, his professional experience rating as a coach had to read zero.

Deke's application for the Bloomfield High opening had been a shot in the dark. He heard about the job late in the spring and sent off a letter. What was there to lose? He was surprised when he was called in for an interview. He was even more surprised when he got the job. Bloomfield High had decided that Deke Warden, experienced or not, was exactly what the Bulldogs needed.

"It's a real challenge, but I think you can handle it," Deke's college coach had told him. "You're readier than your record shows—and that's what I told 'em when they called me from Bloomfield."

Deke knew the challenge. He knew about the towns like Bloomfield, in the western Illinois corn country. He had grown up in a town just like Bloomfield, a hundred miles to the south. His town was every bit as feverish as Bloomfield when it came to dribbling, shooting, and passing a basketball. He had gone no farther than Illinois State, fifty miles to the east, for his college career. Towns like Bloomfield were home to Deke Warden.

The Bloomfield fans, having no professional or collegiate teams to call their own, concentrated all their loyalties on the high-school teams—football in the fall, basketball in the winter, baseball in the spring. Of the three, basketball mattered most. Fierce rivalries had grown up through the years. Victories were savored, and they were relived in the cafés, barber shops, and living rooms of Bloomfield. Defeats went down hard, and they were remembered. The quality of life, as Deke understood full well, was measured by the won-lost record of the basketball team.

Last year in Bloomfield the quality of life had hit a new low. The Bulldogs won less than half their games. Nobody in Bloomfield could remember such disaster. The coach moved on to another job.

At this point, Deke knew almost nothing about the players he was going to have for his first Bloomfield Bulldogs basketball team. He knew nothing about whatever problems had been plaguing the Bulldogs last year. Perhaps there had been a drought of good player material. Perhaps something else. Deke knew only that he had a busy six weeks ahead of him, leading up to the start of practice. He had a lot to learn.

Deke's thoughts were interrupted by the sudden appearance of Sam Kaplin, the owner of the apartment building.

"Everything okay?" Sam asked with a smile, meeting Deke outside the front door.

"Perfect," Deke said. After four years of dormitory living at Illinois State, the small, furnished bachelor apartment seemed a palatial luxury. Located only three blocks from Bloomfield High, Deke was within easy walking distance of the gymnasium where he was going to shape his first basketball team.

Deke had liked the slender gray-haired man with the rimless spectacles from their first meeting, when he came to inspect the apartment two weeks ago. Sam was obviously pleased at the prospect of having the new coach of the Bloomfield Bulldogs as a tenant. He was not going to miss a chance on Deke's moving-in day to cement the relationship. Smiling again, Sam helped Deke carry the last piles of clothing into the apartment.

"What about Bobby Haggard?" Sam asked.

They were walking back to Deke's car together after delivering the last of Deke's belongings.

"Who?"

Sam Kaplin leaned against the rear fender of Deke's car. He ran a hand through his thinning hair. He folded his arms over his chest. And he became the first person to tell Deke about Bobby Haggard.

The slender little redhead, a tenth-grader last year, was a deadeye shooter from the outside, capable of pouring in twenty points or more on a good night. He was a master dribbler, sure-handed, quick, and clever. On defense he was a ball-hawking guard with a talent for theft and interceptions.

"I haven't missed a Bulldog home game in—let's see now, the year of my surgery—fourteen years," Sam said, screwing up his face in a thoughtful frown. "And, believe me, Bobby Haggard is the best we've ever had."

But Bobby Haggard had not finished the season with the Bloomfield Bulldogs last year.

"That was when everything really fell apart—when Bobby quit the team, or got thrown off the team, or whatever happened," Sam said.

Deke listened, certain he was getting the first glimmer of one of the big reasons behind the disastrous season of the basketball team he was inheriting.

"Even before that, though, things weren't good," Sam said. Sam's deep frown stayed in place. The fate of the Bulldogs' basketball team was serious business. "There were stories about the players scrapping among themselves from the very start of the season. Some of the dissension showed during the games, right out there on the court. Bobby was bad about fussing and shouting at anyone who made a mistake. The players didn't like it, not a bit. It showed on their faces. One night I heard a bad scrap in the dressing room myself. I was walking by. I could hear 'em screaming at each other."

"Sounds bad," Deke said.

"Oh, they weren't getting along, no doubt about that. And it showed in the way they played. Even when Bobby was playing—and he really pumped in the points—they weren't able to get together on a winning combination. Bobby might score twenty-five points, but they'd still get whipped by two. Something always went wrong, if you know what I mean."

Deke nodded. "And—"

"And then, all of a sudden, Bobby was off the team." Sam shrugged his shoulders in puzzlement. "Nobody ever explained it."

"What kind of boy is Bobby Haggard?" Deke asked.

Sam smiled. "You hear all kinds of stories," he said.

"Runs with the wrong crowd, I think. You know the sort, out all night, a little drinking, a little pot smoking, maybe. I've heard some of the teachers complaining about his behavior in class. He does crazy things to get attention, gets himself in trouble. Got himself suspended once for something or other." Sam paused. "Some of the teachers live here in the apartments, you know, like you do, because they're close to the school. I hear them talking."

"Bobby Haggard's got a general reputation as a troublemaker then," Deke said. "And it carried over into troublemaking on the team."

"I guess that's about it," Sam said. "But we sure need him on the team."

For Deke, the story from Sam Kaplin was only the first of many. The questions and comments about Bobby Haggard came at Deke from all sides whenever he was recognized as the new basketball coach.

Later the same afternoon a telephone installer, hooking up the wires in Deke's apartment: "If you get Bobby Haggard back, the Bulldogs will be okay."

And that evening, at the Nemo Café on Main Street, Willard Gresham, owner and proprietor, while giving Deke his change at the cash register: "The kid's a little wild, I guess, but with the right kind of guidance he'll come around, and that's what the Bulldogs need—Bobby Haggard."

The next morning, getting his first haircut in Bloomfield, Deke listened to Ellis Findley, peering at Deke through thick glasses while working the clippers: "Nothing can stop the Bulldogs with Bobby Haggard in there.

Never saw anything like the way he shoots in those long ones." And then the question: "Is he going to get everything together this year?"

In the afternoon, in Deke's first encounter with Herbie Foxx, sports director of the Bloomfield radio station: "A good coach can handle Bobby Haggard, and that'll solve all the problems."

There was no mistaking the challenge in Herbie Foxx's statement, and the implicit question as to whether Deke Warden was the man to do the job.

They were seated together in Herbie's office at the station. Deke was keeping an appointment to tape an interview for Herbie's evening sports show. They were waiting for somebody to finish up in the taping studio so they could begin the interview.

"That's why Clair Thornton is gone," Herbie said. He spoke in a clipped, authoritative tone. "Clair Thornton was not able to handle the Bobby Haggard problem."

Deke already had guessed as much. From the talk with Sam Kaplin in front of his apartment to the words of Ellis Findley while he sat in a barber chair, Deke got the message. But until now all of the questions and all of the words of advice had been couched in a friendly tone. Everyone seemed to be wishing Deke well. Not so with Herbie Foxx. The sportscaster was sizing him up and clearly deciding he was not satisfied.

"Do you think you can handle it?" Herbie asked. His expression told Deke that the sportscaster was sure he knew the answer already.

Deke, puzzled and unsettled, shifted his large frame in the chair. He had hoped to find a supporter in the radio station's sports director. Herbie Foxx handled the play-by-play broadcasts of the Bulldogs' games. His remarks were sure to help—or hurt—the image of Deke and his team in the eyes of the Bloomfield fans. Deke and his Bulldogs needed Herbie Foxx on their side.

Deke chose the words of his reply carefully, certain he was going to be asked to repeat them on tape during the interview. "I haven't had a chance to meet any of the players yet," he said. "I'm new here. I've got a lot of work to do, a lot of judgments to make. In the end, the record will have to provide the answer to your question."

Herbie did, to give him credit, phrase the question differently when the tape recorder was running. But the question was there, and Deke felt a sense of relief that he had had the chance in Herbie's office to frame his answer in advance.

From the radio station, Deke drove straight to the high school to seek out Arnie Hamilton, the veteran coach of the Bloomfield Bulldogs.

Deke had heard enough about Bobby Haggard in two days to last a full season, but it all added up to nothing. What he needed now was information from someone who knew what he was talking about. Arnie Hamilton was the man to provide the answers.

The football players were trudging off the practice field at the end of a long afternoon when Deke pulled his car to the curb. Deke got out and stood for a moment watching the long line of dusty, sweaty, weary players on their way to the dressing room.

At the end of the line was Arnie, now jogging slightly and shouting, "C'mon, show a little life."

Deke grinned at the football coach's needling remark.

The players glanced at Arnie and, unsmiling, broke into a leisurely jog designed to satisfy Arnie's demand.

Deke stepped forward and joined Arnie for the last few steps to the field-house door. "Will you have a few minutes after your shower?" Deke asked. "I need to talk to you."

Arnie glanced sideways at Deke and smiled in a knowing way. He patted his ample stomach with his right hand for a moment. Then he said, "You want to ask me about Bobby Haggard."

Deke grinned.

Arnie Hamilton had been the Bloomfield football coach for more than twenty years. He knew his football. Also, he knew the town of Bloomfield. Arnie's smile and his flat statement of fact showed that he was aware of the questions flying at Deke from all directions.

"Sure." Arnie smiled as they stepped inside. "Give me ten or fifteen minutes. Okay?"

Deke walked into the gymnasium to wait. The gymnasium was large, seating more than five thousand. Deke stepped into the center of the court and looked around at the empty seats. He had played here twice as a high schooler—one victory, one loss. Now he was going to be coaching the Bloomfield Bulldogs in this gymnasium. Every one of those seats was going to be filled. The Bloomfield fans were proud of the fact that every game had been a sell-out since construction of the gym ten years ago. Even last year, when the Bulldogs were stumbling through a dreadful season of losses, the fans had turned out and packed the place.

In the emptiness now, Deke could hear the roar of the crowd.

He had heard how the Bloomfield fans cheered Bobby Haggard with a rhythmic chant—"Go-Bobby-Go! Go-Bobby-Go!"

Deke could imagine the effect. A roaring basketball crowd is a mighty force. Enclosed tightly in a gym sealed against the wintry weather, the sound reverberates. The rafters seem to shake. The bricks in the wall seem certain to crumble. The adrenalin flows. Deke knew about it. He had heard his hometown fans roar, "Dunk it, Deke," every time his tall frame left the floor under the basket with the ball in his hand. Deke never denied that the roar gave him a thrill.

Surely the little redhead whose shots from the outside brought the crowd to their feet roaring "Go-Bobby-Go!" felt the same thrill.

"There you are," Arnie called out.

Deke, standing in the center of the court, turned.

Arnie smiled and said, "You're a little early for the first game." Waving a hand at the empty seats, he added, "Not even the first fan is here yet."

Deke dribbled an imaginary ball for two steps and shot it toward the basket. "I played in this gym a couple of times," he said, walking toward Arnie at the sideline.

"I remember you," Arnie said. "You were pretty good."

"Can we go in your office?" Deke asked.

"Sure."

"First of all, he's the best basketball player I've seen in these parts in more than twenty years," Arnie Hamilton said.

Arnie was leaning back in the chair behind his scarred wooden desk. The small office showed the signs of long occupancy. Team pictures in black frames covered one wall. A large homemade calendar, blocking out the weeks of football season, hung on the opposite wall. Already there were illegible scribblings on the calendar noting reminders and goals. Behind Arnie, a photograph of a handsome young man smiled down—a player Arnie had coached at Bloomfield High who went on to become an All-American player in college. The inscription read: "To Arnie Hamilton, who showed me how." The desk in front of Arnie was covered with the litter of his job—yellow notepads, mail, coaching magazines, and sports-page clippings about the Bulldogs' upcoming opponents. Deke recalled the old saying about a littered desk meaning an unlittered mind.

Deke sat in the office's only other chair, leaning forward, elbows on his knees, hands clasped in front of him.

"But Bobby Haggard is a troubled boy," Arnie said slowly, seeming to weigh each word before he spoke. The usual Arnie Hamilton smile, easy and amiable, was missing. Arnie was frowning. "Bobby Haggard is convinced that nobody likes him. As a result, of course, nobody does. Oh, he's got his friends, you know, but they're a bunch with the same problems he has. They're convinced that everybody is looking down on them."

Arnie paused. "Bobby keeps his guard up at all times. He refuses to let anyone get close to him. He won't open up to anyone, won't let anyone be his friend. He thrashes out at people—literally, sometimes—to make sure that he is rejecting them before they can reject him. Simple as that, I'm afraid. He's been a classroom behavioral problem—wild antics to draw attention to himself. He spent a lot of time in punishment study hall last year. Got himself suspended once."

The Arnie Hamilton smile returned, and he said, "I'm not a psychologist—although every coach ought to be one—but I think that Bobby Haggard has got what they call a self-worth problem. He holds himself in low esteem. So, naturally, he assumes everyone else does, too.

He thrashes out to prove it's not so or doesn't matter."

"Basketball seems the perfect answer for him," Deke said. "Why in the world . . . ?"

"Should be," Arnie said. "I agree with you. One of the great benefits of high-school sports is the chance for a kid to prove himself outstanding, or at least adequate, and to belong to the group—be a part of the team, somebody important."

"But it hasn't worked out that way with Bobby Haggard—"

"No, it hasn't. Being able to score twenty points or more in front of a cheering crowd should do the job. How can he feel inferior when everybody is shouting his name? How can he fail to *belong* in a group that needs his twenty points? By refusing to allow himself to belong, that's how."

Deke started to speak, but Arnie continued. "And to be honest about the matter, the other players aren't helping. If Bobby Haggard were a new kid in town, they'd give him a chance. They're not bad kids. You'll see. But they've put up with Bobby Haggard's refusal to fit in ever since they were in kindergarten. They figure they know him. They figure he's not going to change. And they know they don't like him."

Arnie frowned thoughtfully. "He comes from a family that's not, well, not well off. He always was the kid with the old secondhand bicycle when the others had new ones. His clothes were never quite the match of the others. You know what I mean." Arnie paused. "Hell, lots of kids overcome that kind of handicap. But Bobby hasn't. His parents don't help much. I guess that about the best you can say for them is that they're indifferent. I never even saw them at a basketball game when the whole town was screaming his name."

Deke nodded. Bobby Haggard's background was clear enough to him. He understood. Deke had never had such specific reasons for feeling he was an outsider. But he knew the empty, lonely feeling of trying to belong—and fearing rejection. Everyone knows the feeling. Everyone has the experience, with or without good reason, at some time in his life. Most find a way to overcome their fears and let the world come in.

For Deke, an understanding coach and his own ability to dribble, pass, and shoot better than anyone else provided the key to success. His mind flashed back to the day—really, the only day—he had felt himself a lonely outsider on a basketball team.

Deke was a tenth-grader, turning out to sign up for the basketball team for the first time. He had lived in the town all his life, but he was new to the high school. He was surrounded by boys he had known all his life, but they seemed different standing in the gym on that first day. They all seemed to belong to the team. The older ones had played one or two years. They were sure of themselves. That was understandable. But even the beginners, who were Deke's classmates in the tenth grade, seemed to be fitting into the group easily. They did not appear to be worried or frightened or nervous. Deke alone was the one on the outside trying to break into the circle. The others, it seemed, were all in the group already.

The coach, with wisdom Deke only appreciated much later, intervened. "Donald Kensington Warden," he intoned in a solemn voice reading the roll call of the players signing up.

Deke lifted a hand.

The coach glanced at him. "That's quite a name," he said. "We can't call you all of that."

There were chuckles. Deke felt a flare of embarrassment.

"We can't call you Don," the coach said. "We've already got one Don—and we can't stand another one like him."

There was laughter, and Deke felt a little easier.

"Can't call you Ken either," the coach said. "We've got one of those, too—and he's as bad as Don."

More laughter.

"Donald Kensington Warden," the coach pronounced again. "D.K. D.K. Warden. Deke, we'll call you Deke."

From that day on, Donald Kensington Warden was Deke Warden. The ploy, Deke knew now, was an old one. But it worked. Nicknames are a sign of belonging. Deke Warden stuck with the team. Idly Deke wondered what Bobby Haggard's middle name was.

Then he pulled himself back to the present. "What happened last year?" Deke asked. "Bobby didn't finish the season with the team. I've already heard so much from so many—"

"It was a mess all the way," Arnie said. He leaned back in his chair and locked his hands behind his head. "There was friction all the way—oh, worse than that—and most of it caused by Bobby. For one thing, he called one of the black kids on the team a nigger in the dressing room once. They almost got into a fistfight. Couple of players got in between them just in time to stop it. You're lucky the kid has graduated. But the other players haven't forgotten, you can bet. Especially Benjy Holman. He's black, sure to be your starting center. And Bobby was bad, too, about ridiculing his teammates—for a fumble or a missed shot—right out there on the court in front of the crowd. You can imagine—"

"Yes, I can," Deke said. "What did Clair Thornton do?"

Arnie sighed. "I think that Clair Thornton mishandled the situation terribly." He paused, then added almost parenthetically, "I'm not sure I could have done any better, but the fact remains that Clair Thornton failed. Oh, I'm not talking about the won-lost record, although it certainly was miserable. I'm talking about the coaching failure with a player who needed purpose and direction. There's more to coaching than teaching the mechanics of a game. We're supposed to help the boys learn the rules of living. I think Clair Thornton forgot about that."

"What led up to Bobby's leaving the team?"

"In a nutshell, Thornton threatened to bench Bobby if he didn't behave. Bobby, of course, took the threat as a dare. He told Thornton he'd quit the team if Thornton benched him. Well, Thornton had painted himself into a corner. He couldn't let Bobby get away with a threat of his own. So Thornton benched Bobby—more to prove his point, show him who was boss, than anything else, which was a serious mistake, I think. With that, the die was cast. Bobby quit."

"Whew!" Deke said with a whistle.

"The fans all blamed Clair Thornton, and Herbie Foxx

tore after him like a bulldog. You've met Herbie, I guess."

Deke raised an eyebrow at the mention of the sportscaster's name. "Yes, I've met him, and it wasn't pleasant. I wanted to ask you—"

Arnie smiled. "I should've warned you," he said. "Herbie not only handles the play-by-play broadcasts and has a very influential evening sports show, but he considers himself the appointed watchdog for the fans and, I think, also considers himself a smarter coach than any we've ever had."

"He was downright antagonistic with me."

"Herbie takes full credit, if credit is the right word, for running Clair Thornton out of Bloomfield, and he had his own candidate to succeed Thornton. Needless to say, it was not you. He took it as a personal slap in the face when you were hired. Simple as that, I'm afraid."

"Uh-huh, I see," Deke said.

Arnie smiled and slapped a hand on the desk top. "Well, I assume your college coach told you the job was a challenge."

Deke looked up in surprise. "Yes," he said, "but he never mentioned the name of Bobby Haggard. Not even the name of Herbie Foxx."

"Welcome to Bloomfield High," Arnie announced.

The first instant of the first meeting with Bobby Haggard delivered a jolt to Deke Warden.

To Deke's horror, he felt an immediate and sharp dislike for the slender redhead. The cocky half grin, almost a sneer, told Deke more about the problems of Bobby Haggard than all the words from Arnie Hamilton and the others. The arrogant glint in Bobby's eyes seemed to dare Deke to be, of all things, friendly.

The meeting was no accident. Deke's first order of business on this first full day of classes had been to visit the administrative offices. He looked up Bobby Haggard's classroom schedule. Then he positioned himself in the corridor to meet Bobby when the bell rang at ten o'clock for the change in classes.

This seemed the perfect arrangement to Deke. Clearly, a casual encounter, a chance meeting—even if staged—was preferable to a formal one. Deke wanted an opportunity to size up the boy. And he wanted Bobby Haggard to have a chance to size up the new coach of the Bulldogs. But Deke did not want to discuss last year, or even this year, in the first meeting. If Bobby Haggard was fast with a rejection, Deke was determined not to give him the chance. The five-minute break between classes guaranteed a brief meeting. The milling crowds of students changing classes provided exactly the easy, informal circumstances that Deke wanted.

"You're Bobby Haggard," Deke said, falling into step with him.

"Yeah," Bobby said. He glanced up at Deke, towering over him.

Deke saw the boy's guard go up. His expression raised the wall. It was automatic, a reflex born of years of habit. Bobby did not even wait to find out who was speaking to him. He was going to expect nothing, and he was going to accept nothing. He was saying, with his eyes and the half grin, that he wanted nothing—and make no mistake about it.

Startled, Deke felt his friendly smile start to fade in the face of the unpleasant, almost antagonistic, response Bobby Haggard put forward.

"I'm Deke Warden." With a conscious effort, Deke held the smile in place as they walked along together.

"Hi," Bobby replied. He turned his face back to the

front and walked along as if he did not care whether Deke trailed along or not.

At five feet, seven inches, Bobby was twelve inches shorter than Deke, a long way from the height most basketball players need for success, even at the high-school level. He was thin but well-proportioned, probably stronger than his size indicated. He was broad-shouldered and narrow-hipped, built for the speed and shiftiness needed by the outstanding back-court basketball player. Even walking leisurely in the corridor, with his books carried easily in one hand, Bobby gave the impression of quick, flittering, unpredictable movement. Deke had seen the quality before. All the good small basketball players had it. They ran circles around larger players. They turned their smallness into an advantage.

"I'm the new basketball coach."

"Yeah, I know." Bobby spoke indifferently, still staring straight ahead.

They walked several steps without speaking. Deke struggled to fight down his instant dislike. The experience was a rare one for him, and it was not pleasant. Deke Warden got along with everyone. He was not able to remember ever meeting anyone who gave him such a sudden feeling of hostility. Especially an athlete, accustomed to the need for friendliness as translated into teamwork. The feeling worried Deke. Coaches are supposed to like their players. Coaches *must* like their players. How could a coach function effectively with a boy he did not like? Sure, everyone likes some people better than others, but almost everyone has some likeable traits, surely even Bobby Haggard, when you get to know him. If Bobby Haggard always gave off these kinds of signals, no wonder he had trouble last year with the coach, his teammates, his classmates, and his teachers. If there's a likeable boy behind that wall, Deke thought, he's going to be hard to find. The guard is up; the wall is high and thick.

"You played some basketball last year, didn't you?" Deke asked casually.

Bobby gave Deke a sideways glance. "Some," he said.

"We'll be starting practice in a little over a month," Deke said.

Bobby said nothing.

Deke was about to add, "I hope you're planning on coming out for the team." But he stopped himself. He decided to say nothing. This was not the time to seek a commitment from Bobby. Rightly or wrongly, Deke got the feeling that Bobby was waiting for an invitation, however vague, so he could reply with a shrug. Deke did not want to box him into issuing a refusal or even the hint of a refusal to come. If Bobby was going to close all doors, he would have to do so later.

"Do they call you Red?" Deke asked easily.

The question was logical enough. Bobby's hair was a light red, almost orange. He was overdue for a date with the barber. His hair covered his ears and touched his collar in the back. He had the light skin of a redhead but none of the freckles that usually complete the picture.

"I don't like to be called Red," Bobby said without looking at Deke.

They were nearing the end of the corridor, where

Deke knew Bobby was going to be turning into a classroom.

"What's your middle name?" Deke asked suddenly.

The cocky half grin vanished, leaving only a blank stare of puzzlement. "What?"

"Your middle name," Deke repeated. "What's your middle name?"

"Witherspoon. Why?"

"Robert Witherspoon Haggard," Deke said. "A very dignified name."

Deke walked away without another word, leaving Bobby to enter the classroom, his face still showing signs of confusion.

Turning a corner and heading down the stairs toward his office, Deke smiled. Robert Witherspoon Haggard would not produce a nickname like Deke, but at least the question wiped away that cocky expression for a moment.

The five weeks leading up to the start of practice whirled by for Deke Warden. As a new coach, he had more than the usual list of preseason tasks to perform. There were his own players to meet. There were their records from last season to study. There were other teams to study, too—the opponents on the Bulldogs' schedule, all new to Deke. There were practice sessions to chart.

There were public appearances, too, for the new basketball coach. Everybody in Bloomfield wanted to see, meet, and hear Deke Warden.

Deke addressed luncheon meetings of the three

Bloomfield civic clubs. At each of them, the introduction of Deke Warden was greeted by a prolonged standing ovation. Deke was taken aback, then troubled, by the outbursts of enthusiasm. These people were the Bloomfield Bulldogs' fans, and they already were counting the victories they were sure the new coach was going to deliver. Deke began to feel the first twinges of the pressures that all coaches live with.

At each of the three luncheons, too, he was asked about Bobby Haggard during the question-and-answer sessions following his remarks. He gave them all the same answer: "At this point, I can't venture a guess about any player."

Deke gave the same answer to Herbie Foxx in a taped interview the week before the start of practice.

The answer was a true one.

Deke had not seen Bobby Haggard again, except for an occasional nodded greeting in the corridors. Unlike some of the other players, Bobby did not drop by Deke's office to visit during the weeks before the start of practice. And Deke did not go out of his way to engage Bobby in conversation.

The idea that Bobby might not come out for the team never entered Deke's mind. True, Bobby had quit the team in a huff last year. There had been sharp conflict with the coach. Now there was a new coach. There had been angry words with his teammates. Many of those teammates were coming back this year. With a lesser player, the social pressure of his peers might have kept him away. But Bobby Haggard was an extraordinary basketball player. He was blessed with a remarkable talent for the game and had honed the talent, through hours of practice, into a vastly superior skill. Nobody worked that hard and played that well, Deke knew, without loving the game. No, Bobby Haggard would turn out for the team when the day for signing up arrived. Deke had no doubts.

Deke felt, too, that basketball offered Bobby his best chance to find—what was it that Arnie Hamilton called it?—self-worth. Perhaps Bobby saw the same possibilities. He was no dummy. He might not use the same term, self-worth, but he hardly could fail to see what basketball might mean to him.

For right now, Deke's tactic with Bobby Haggard was simple: hands off. Treat him like every other student who might become a member of the basketball team.

But the fact was, Bobby Haggard was not long in showing that he was *not* like every other student. Before the end of the second week of classes, Bobby was serving time in the punishment study hall for cutting a class.

The report worried Deke, but he never considered discussing the trouble with Bobby. After all, Bobby was not on Deke's basketball team. Nobody was, at this early date. Bobby had not even given Deke the first indication he intended to play basketball. No, Deke decided quickly, he had no business intruding at this point. Maybe later, if the need arose, but not now.

But Deke did, quietly and without comment to anyone, visit the administrative office and read the record. He copied down the names of the two boys caught skipping a class with Bobby. Right now they meant nothing to Deke—Phil Metzger and Bill Hainey. But Deke would have to know them well if he was going to have a chance of winning the battle for Bobby. They were the boys who passed for friends with Bobby. They were the ones who, probably, Bobby would have to leave behind. Bobby's circle of friends did not have to be confined to the basketball team. Deke's own best friend and dormitory roommate in college had not been an athlete. But in order to measure up to the standards Deke wanted his team to have, Bobby would need friends who measured up, too. "The wrong crowd," Sam Kaplin had called Bobby's friends. Bobby needed the right crowd.

The other players Deke met in the opening days of the school year lifted his spirits.

For Deke, the most exciting was Benjy Holman, the team's only black player, who was returning for his senior season as the Bulldogs' center.

Standing six feet, six inches, he was one inch shorter than Deke. The two of them towered over the other students when they chatted in the corridor during a break between classes.

Benjy probably was going to grow another inch or two before he was finished. His lanky frame was bound to fill out with more weight in the form of muscle. But more than Benjy's size impressed Deke. Deke saw in Benjy's easy movements the same trait he himself had enjoyed —remarkably good coordination for a player of his size. Benjy clearly had everything he needed to be an outstanding player this year at Bloomfield High, and beyond in college.

Deke vowed to put in some special work with the tall

center in the one season he was going to have him with the Bulldogs. The first days of practice would reveal Benjy's strong points and weak points. Those first drills would provide a reading on Benjy's abilities. Then, if Benjy agreed, Deke was ready to spend time with him in the evenings or late afternoons after practice—working on shooting, timing, and footwork. Whatever weaknesses Benjy had as a basketball player could be overcome. Deke was sure of it. His strengths as a player could be made all the greater in the course of a few tutoring sessions. Deke's instincts told him Benjy had the makings of a great basketball player. And Deke thought he saw in Benjy's steady gaze and his quiet, serious manner the dedication needed to reach full potential.

The combination of Bobby Haggard pumping them in from the outside and Benjy Holman dominating the backboards on the inside spelled a lethal one-two scoring punch. The talents complemented each other. Bobby's long shots were sure to pull out the guards, freeing Benjy. And Benjy's work under the basket was sure to pull the guards back in, freeing Bobby. Deke smiled at the thought.

"Drop it," Deke told himself finally. "For a coach who has yet to see a player take his first shot, you're counting up a lot of points."

Deke tried, too, not to think about the story of Bobby calling a teammate nigger in the dressing room last season—a scene that Benjy Holman undoubtedly had witnessed and surely remembered.

Aside from Benjy, the only other senior on the team, also returning from the starting five last year, was Skipper Denham. He appeared in Deke's office one afternoon, shook hands solemnly, and extended a welcome on behalf of Bloomfield High. Handsome with a strong chin, a narrow, straight nose, and short, curly black hair, Skipper was a serious boy, mature for his age, president of the Student Council, and the undisputed leader of the team.

Deke returned Skipper's greeting warmly. Here was the player who might lead the other Bulldogs into acceptance of Bobby Haggard.

In pairs or alone, in chance encounters in the corridors or in the casual drop-in visits in his office, Deke met them all during September and the early days of October—the proven lettermen, the anxious hopefuls, the sure and unsure.

The big day arrived.

Deke had posted the notice on the Bloomfield High bulletin boards the previous week: Basketball sign-up, Monday 3:30 P.M., gymnasium locker room.

Now the new coach of the Bloomfield Bulldogs stood in the door to the locker room watching the boys who were going to be the players on his first high-school basketball team.

Deke, wearing the gray sweat suit he planned to make his uniform for the practice sessions, might have been one of the players. He was, he reflected, barely four years older than some of them. This time last year, in fact, he was showing up for the first day of practice as a player at Illinois State.

Across the room, at a long table, a student manager was passing a clipboard among the boys. They were signing up—name, age, class, height, weight. Then the manager took the clipboard back and filled in two figures—locker assignment and uniform number—and passed out the baskets containing the practice suits. The players were taking their baskets and hunting up their lockers and beginning to change clothes for the first drill of the season.

Deke noticed the boys around the room casting quick, questioning glances at him as they drew their equipment and changed clothes. There was an uncertain expression even on the face of the self-assured Skipper Denham. Deke understood the glances. He knew the players' feelings. His own days as a player were not so far removed. All of them, veterans and newcomers alike, were wondering about the new coach. Deke met their questioning looks with a smile and a nod.

Deke's gaze moved around the room until he found the player he was looking for, the slender little redhead at a locker in the corner, seated on the bench, tying his shoes.

Bobby Haggard, alone and apart from the others, was here.

By tip-off time of the opening game of the season, eleven days later, Deke Warden was elated, troubled, and—for reasons only partly related to his players—exhausted.

The crowd was streaming into the Bloomfield High gym, filling the bleachers on both sides of the court. There was going to be standing room only, as usual. The Bulldogs' fans, always loyal, always enthusiastic, always optimistic, had extra reason to be excited tonight. Not only was this the first game of the season, always a moment of high hopes. Beyond that, a new coach was at the helm. A better world was opening up for the Bulldogs.

If more proof was needed, there was Bobby Haggard taking his warm-up shots. Bobby Haggard was back with the Bulldogs.

Already some of the fans in the crowd were shouting the chant—"Go-Bobby-Go! Go-Bobby-Go!"

Deke stood at the bench, watching his Bulldogs in their bright green warm-up suits run through patterns of dribbling, passing, and shooting.

At the other end of the court, the Appleton Falcons were going through their paces.

The bright overhead lights of the gym bathed the court in whiteness, leaving not a single shadow. The polished floor gleamed in the light.

Under the bleachers in the far corner, out of sight, a combo from the Bloomfield High band blared a fight song.

In the broadcast booth, high above the bleachers opposite him, Deke saw Herbie Foxx leaning into a microphone. Herbie's mouth was working furiously as he described the rebirth of the Bloomfield Bulldogs as a basketball power. Deke could imagine the words.

Deke turned back to his players on the court. They were weaving through from left and right, taking the handoffs from Benjy Holman under the basket and laying the ball up. They looked good. They were smooth and confident. They had grasped the theory behind Deke's style of play without trouble in the ten days of practice. The skills to execute the plays were there. They were ready and should be winners.

But for Deke, the previous night had been restless, a

series of frightening dreams broken only by periods of sleepless tossing in his bed.

In the first dream, his Bulldogs went down to defeat by the score of 50–0. The Bulldogs not only lost; they failed even to score. Every shot went awry. Every pass was intercepted. Players fumbled at every turn. They bumped into each other time and again. The roaring boos of the angry fans were ringing in Deke's ears when he awoke, his heart pounding.

In a later dream, inexplicably, Deke was on horseback, racing for his life across the prairie with a crowd of screaming Indians on their ponies in pursuit, spraying arrows all around him. Miraculously, none of the arrows hit home. Deke awoke breathless.

Staring through the darkness toward the ceiling of his bedroom, Deke wondered what the dreams meant. But he knew. This was his first game as a coach. What if he lost the game? What if his team lost every game? What if they never won at all? He told himself that his fears were not really ridiculous. Somebody loses every time out. What if Deke's team were the loser—every time?

Finally, Deke got out of bed. He walked into the kitchen and drank a glass of milk. He told himself that his nervousness was silly. But the nervousness stayed.

And now, on the sideline, he felt the weariness brought on by the night of tension. He felt the urge to stretch his arms. He tried to stifle a yawn and failed. He kept his hands, which were trembling, thrust in his trousers pockets.

The ten days of practice had heightened Deke's hopes, and they also had given him cause for worry.

Bobby Haggard was every bit the basketball player everybody said he was. That was obvious from the first moment of the first practice session. Bobby walked onto the court, dribbled easily across the edge of the keyhole, turned, leaped, shot, and—swish! The high, arching shot dropped through the net without touching the rim. Every movement was perfect, from the first caressing touch of the basketball to the lovely sound of the ball socking the net.

Benjy Holman proved to have all the fluid movements Deke had seen in their first meeting, plus a good shooting eye. Rangy, with good jumping ability, he dominated the backboards. His good timing made him deadly on tip-ins. His accuracy with shots from ten to fifteen feet out was an unexpected benefit. Deke worked with Benjy to develop a quicker release on his shots. Three times in the ten days of practice, Deke brought Benjy back to the gym at night for tutoring. With Deke guarding, Benjy fired away. Benjy worked hard, and he listened and learned.

The inside-outside combination of Bobby Haggard and Benjy Holman gave the Bulldogs a whipsaw attack sure to cut through any defense.

Skipper Denham at one forward position and Dennis North at the other were adequate. Skipper was heavy-footed and slow. But he was steady, sure-handed, and possessed a good shot from the corner. Dennis was a scrapper capable of dribbling through for a lay-up at any time. Ken Flaherty at the other guard position with

Bobby complete the first five. Ken was neither the ball handler nor the shooter that Bobby was, but he had no trouble reclaiming the job he had held the previous season, beating out Chris Santini during the ten days of practice. Chris, who had moved into Bobby's guard position when the little redhead had left the team last year, was a strong substitute, capable of playing any position except Benjy's center slot. Fortunately for all, Chris's easygoing manner, quick to laugh and joke, enabled him to slide back into the role of substitute without bad feelings.

On the surface, Deke had a dream team. He knew it. The Bulldogs had two potential all-staters—Bobby and Benjy—and not a single serious weakness in the lineup.

But beneath the surface, Deke sensed the currents of trouble. Bobby's cocky half grin never left his face. The other players ignored Bobby. They did not speak to him or look at him. The huzzahs that went up when Skipper or Ken dunked a shot in a practice scrimmage were not heard when Bobby scored. The players turned and ran back down the court after a Bobby Haggard field goal as if nothing had happened.

And all the while Bobby dared them with his eyes to say the first word.

Deke found himself relieved that the first word never was said—either by Bobby or anyone else—during the ten days of practice. An uneasy peace was better than war.

Twice Deke tried to set the stage for smoothing out the relationships by talking with players—first Benjy, then Skipper.

He was driving Benjy home from one of their nighttime tutoring sessions.

"Got time for a root beer?"

"Sure."

Deke pulled into a drive-in, and they ordered from the car.

"You and Bobby, the inside and the outside of the attack, are going to make a terrific combination," Deke said. He hoped that by mixing the mention of Bobby with a compliment for Benjy, he might strike a responsive chord.

Benjy seemed to recognize immediately where Deke's conversation was heading. He was silent a moment. Then he said, "Coach, I don't like the dude. I've got my reasons. They're good reasons. He doesn't like me either. But I'll play the game with him. When we're on the court in a game, you'll think I love him like a brother. But I don't."

"It'd help," Deke said, "if you and the others gave him a chance to like you."

"He's the one who doesn't give chances," Benjy said. "Maybe you ought to talk to him."

A day later, with Skipper Denham at a table in the cafeteria during the lunch period, the words were different but the answer the same: "Coach, we don't like him, and he doesn't like us. He's bad news. Always has been. But for the good of the team we'll play with him."

Deke came out of the talks wondering if the bigger problem was Bobby's arrogant grin and the history of insulting remarks, or if it was now the players' refusal to give Bobby another chance. Somewhere between the two problems there was a solution. But right now the only result of the two problems was that Bobby was left on the outside.

The buzzer sounded, and Deke stepped forward at the sideline to greet his players coming off the court for the last moment before the start of the game.

The roar of the crowd rolled down out of the bleachers all around him. The combo still was blaring away from its position out of sight under the bleachers. The cheerleaders were skipping at the center of the court, clapping their hands in time to the music. The lights seemed brighter than ever.

Deke dropped to one knee and leaned into the group of players around him—the five starters standing in front, and the substitutes behind them.

Suddenly Deke was no longer tired. He did not want to stretch his arms. He was not trying to stifle a yawn. His hands were not trembling.

In the center of the group six pairs of hands—Deke's and the starters'—gripped, pumped once, and released.

"Go get 'em," Deke said, and he stepped back to watch his first basketball team take the court for the first time.

The Bulldogs crushed the Appleton Falcons by a score of 61-43.

To Deke's horror, the Falcons had scored the first field goal. They were leading 2-0 with the game less than a minute old. Deke shivered at the memory of his dream. Could it be?

But the Bulldogs got the next eight straight points in short order. Bobby swiped the ball at mid-court, dribbled a couple of steps, leaped, pumped—and scored to tie the count at 2-2. When the Falcons came back, Benjy grabbed a rebound and passed off to Ken Flaherty. Ken shot a long pass downcourt to Skipper, and Skipper laid it in for a 4-2 lead. Then Skipper intercepted a Falcons' pass and lofted a high sailer that Benjy caught at basket level and tipped in, raising the count to 6-2. The Falcons, quickly becoming rattled, lost the ball out-of-bounds on a bad pass. Seconds later Bobby fired in his second field goal. The score stood at 8-2.

And that was only the beginning.

Deke sat on the bench, leaning forward, elbows on knees, hands clasped in front of him, watching the smooth machinery of his basketball team. The outside-inside combination of Bobby and Benjy was tearing the Falcons apart. When the Falcons expanded their zone defense to stymie Bobby, Benjy took in high passes and poked the ball in the basket. When the Falcons retrenched to gang up on the rangy Benjy under the basket, Bobby fired away from the outside.

The potency of Bobby and Benjy opened up opportunities for the other Bulldogs. The Falcons' defense, torn between Benjy scoring from under the basket and Bobby scoring from the outside, left Skipper open in the corner, Ken free to drive in for lay-ups, and Dennis North open for his set shots.

On defense, the story again was Bobby and Benjy. Bobby's quick hands drove the Falcons' dribblers frantic. And when the Falcons succeeded in getting off a shot, Benjy was there, leaping, pulling the ball off the backboard to start the Bulldogs toward another field goal.

Late in the first quarter, and again early in the second quarter, the Falcons' coach called time-out. He was trying to settle his team down. He was changing his offense to try to elude Bobby at mid-court. He was telling his players to wait for the sure shot. The tall, black center was getting all the rebounds when they missed. The coach was trying to revise his defense to slow down the scoring by the rushing Bulldogs.

But nothing worked.

The Bulldogs' power, speed, and shooting accuracy ran around, over, and past the outclassed Falcons.

All around the gym, the Bloomfield fans were on their feet, roaring. The pandemonium started when the Bulldogs made their run of eight points early in the game. The fans sensed a runaway victory. Their dreams for the season were coming true. Last year was over. This year was a new start. They were enjoying it. The volume of their cheers rose with each additional point. The chant—"Go-Bobby-Go! Go-Bobby-Go!"—rang out every time the redhead turned, jumped, and fired.

So complete was the rout that Deke began feeding substitutes into the game midway through the second quarter. First, Chris Santini took the floor, replacing Bobby, who had scored fourteen points in a little over ten minutes. Even Chris, weak on long shots, got a hot hand and scored three field goals from the outside.

One by one, Deke fed other substitutes from the bench into the game. By half time, only Benjy remained of the first five on the court, and the Bulldogs were leading by a score of 42-26.

In the dressing room at the intermission, Deke moved among the players, quietly extending compliments and offering advice on how to avoid in the second half the few miscues of the first half.

His Bulldogs had, in fact, played virtually errorless ball.

"How'm I doin'?" Bobby asked with the crooked half grin in place.

Deke grimaced at the use of the first person singular. In the quiet of the dressing room, Deke was sure the others heard Bobby's question and the *I* instead of *we*.

Deke glared at Bobby for a moment. If anything was going to break down the wall between Bobby and the other players, it was going to be a big victory. Nothing makes buddies like succeeding together. But now one ill-worded remark reminded everyone in the room that, scorer of fourteen points or no, they disliked Bobby Haggard.

"We're going great so far," Deke said. He resisted the urge to underscore the *we* with his tone of voice. Then he added, "Nice shooting, Bobby, and nice defense, too."

The players were toweling off, and Deke let them rest. He had been pleased with the first half. His Bulldogs were looking stronger than he had hoped. True, the Falcons, never considered to be a strong contender, were turning out to be weaker than expected. But the Bulldogs were doing everything right. They looked like a genuine powerhouse basketball team.

"We're winning big, and it's a good feeling," Deke told the team in the final seconds before returning to the court.

The players, slumped on benches in front of lockers, towels draped around their necks, looked up at him.

Deke decided that it was silly to warn them about

the dangers of a letdown. They were not going to lose to the Falcons. The players knew it as well as Deke. From his own playing days, Deke remembered how ridiculous a coach sounded warning a vastly superior team that the hopelessly outclassed opponent might yet rise up and whip them.

But he had a word of caution to deliver. "Teams develop habits, just like individuals," he said. "There are good habits and there are bad habits. For a basketball team, good habits—alert, aggressive play, careful attention to detail—spell victory. Bad habits—poor passing, mental errors, careless ball handling—spell defeat."

He paused and glanced at the faces around the room. The sober, serious Skipper was concentrating on Deke's every word. Benjy, expressionless, was sitting forward, watching Deke. Chris showed the excitement he was feeling after taking the court and scoring three field goals. Bobby's expression caused Deke to pause. With his eyes, Bobby was saying, "We all know that you think you've got to give us this bull. Just get it over with."

Deke continued. "When you're winning big, the way we are, there's a tendency to get a little sloppy. And that's how sloppy habits develop. And sloppy habits will lose a lot of games against the tougher teams than the Falcons we're going to be playing throughout the season. Play the second half as if we're trailing, and we'll be developing the good habits that will pay off later."

The Falcons were no better in the second half. And the Bulldogs, with substitutes playing most of the way, steamrollered past them without the first hint of a letdown.

At the finish, Bobby had eighteen points, having played less than half of the thirty-two minutes of the game.

Benjy wound up with seventeen points. And, to Deke's delight, Benjy got three field goals with jumpers from more than ten feet out. The night sessions with the two of them on the practice court had paid off. Benjy's skills included more than height and jumping ability for tip-ins.

So much for nightmares, Deke thought, as he walked off the court and glanced up at the final score in lights: Not 50-0 for the opponent, but 61-43 in the Bulldogs' favor.

Deke knew that the Indians were not going to be chasing him on horseback through his dreams tonight.

As for the specter of Bobby Haggard's crooked half grin, well, that would wait till morning.

The opponents fell, one by one.

The Bloomfield Bulldogs rolled over their first seven foes, marking up easy victories.

Bobby Haggard was averaging a fraction more than twenty-one points a game. The quick-firing little sharp-shooter was unstoppable. Neither a zone defense nor a man-to-man effort bottled him up for long. Opponents tried double-teaming him. It didn't work. Opponents put chasers on him in an effort to harass and knock him off stride. But that didn't work either. No matter what, Bobby shook free, leaped, fired his high arching shot and—swish!—kept on scoring.

Deke grew accustomed to the roaring chant of the Bloomfield fans, "Go-Bobby-Go! Go-Bobby-Go!"

Bobby was worth more than his points to the Bulldogs. The mere threat of his shooting was paying off. A defense bulging outward to try to contain Bobby left gaps elsewhere.

On the inside, under the basket, Benjy Holman was finding himself open time and again. He was getting the split second of freedom he needed to pour in the points. Deadly with a hook shot and reliable on tip-ins, Benjy was averaging better than sixteen points a game, almost double his production of the year before. He owed much of the improvement to his own growth and development. As a senior, a year older, he was bigger and stronger than the previous year. He owed much, too, to the tips he picked up in the after-hours tutoring sessions with Deke. The combination of the two—his own growth and the knowledge he gained from Deke—added up to increased confidence. He moved with greater authority as the games rolled by. But the fact remained that Benjy owed much of his success to the menace of Bobby Haggard out around the edge of the keyhole, drawing the attention of the defense.

Skipper Denham was enjoying the same kind of freedom, again thanks to the threat of Bobby's outside shooting. He was getting open in the corner for his one-hand push shots, and he was finding empty space in the lanes under the backboards to dribble through and put in a lay-up. Skipper was averaging twelve points a game.

Bobby Haggard was the catalyst of the Bulldogs' attack, the biggest point producer and, as the box scores never revealed, responsible in a very real way for many of the points scored by his teammates.

On defense, Bobby's quick feet and quick hands robbed the opponents of points. In one game alone, Bobby stole the ball seven times, with pass interceptions, fumble recoveries, and outright theft from the hands of a befuddled opponent. Deke was so sure the achievement was a record that he called the State High School Athletic Association office, only to be told that such statistics were not recorded.

Not a one of the Bulldogs' first seven opponents finished within ten points. Most were a dozen or more points behind at the end, despite Deke's liberal use of substitutes.

Across the state, in Peoria, Chicago, and Springfield, the sportswriters and sportscasters saw the scores. They were beginning to call Deke for interviews. They were busy writing and talking about the rebirth of the Bloomfield Bulldogs. A new age was opening for Bloomfield basketball under the leadership of the new young coach named Deke Warden and behind the unerring jump shots of the slender redhead named Bobby Haggard. "Phoenix rises from the ashes," one of the sportswriters wrote.

In Bloomfield, the fans were ecstatic. The crowds at the games, always a sellout whether the team was winning or losing down through the years, were larger than ever. For the seventh game the first tickets had been sold and the first seats occupied shortly after four o'clock in the afternoon. By game time, three and a half hours later, the lobby was jammed with fans who had not the faintest chance of getting a seat. But they stayed anyway. Some settled for listening to the loudspeaker descriptions of the game they could not see. Others held transistor radios to their ears for Herbie Foxx's play-by-play account of the game. Seeing the game or not, they were there, which was the important thing.

For the out-of-town games, fans were setting up caravans of cars to accompany the Bulldogs' team van. Thirty-two cars had followed the Bulldogs to their sixth game—and their sixth victory.

"That's too bad, winning all those games," Arnie Hamilton told Deke with a smile. "A smart coach loses a few when he first comes on the scene. That way the fans aren't expecting too much. Then you can afford to lose a few later."

Deke knew there was more truth than jest in Arnie's good-natured remark.

Everywhere that Deke went in Bloomfield he was greeted with shouts and smiling waves and cheers and outstretched hands.

On the face of it, Deke Warden, a rookie coach, and the Bloomfield Bulldogs, a hapless bunch last year, were riding high. But Deke knew the Bulldogs were a troubled team. More and more, while the victories piled up, Deke found his time and thoughts occupied by the ominous signals he was receiving at every turn.

Most of the storm warnings were hardly major incidents. They were small episodes. All teams have them. Members of a basketball team are too close to each other to avoid having one rub another the wrong way once in a while. But in the case of the Bulldogs, they all totaled up to serious trouble looming on the horizon.

A couple of weeks before, during a practice scrimmage, Bobby had sprung toward a pass and succeeded in deflecting the ball toward the sideline. Both Bobby and Dennis North scampered after the loose ball. Dennis, coming in at a sharp angle, swung a hip into the low-running Bobby. The blow sent Bobby sprawling on the floor.

Deke could not be sure that Dennis had butted Bobby intentionally. Such collisions do occur in the hot pursuit of a loose ball on the basketball court. But there was no doubt in Bobby's mind. He turned over from the painful fall with anger sparkling in his eyes. Getting to his feet, he glared at Dennis. But he said nothing.

Deke noticed, and surely Bobby did, too, that Dennis turned away without so much as a mumbled, "Sorry."

Minutes later Bobby retaliated, but in a different way. He stole the ball out of Dennis's hands—as nifty a theft as Deke ever had seen—and dribbled away. Bobby's quick hands and his speed afoot left Dennis standing flat-footed and empty-handed. Dennis's face first showed befuddlement. One moment he had the ball; the next, he didn't. Then, realizing what had happened, his expression changed to one of embarrassment. Bobby, with the cocky half grin on his face, laughed over his shoulder at Dennis as he dribbled away.

Of the two blows, Bobby's was the more devastating, no question.

However, some of the danger signals were, indeed, major ones.

In their fifth game, against Clarendon Lake, Bobby had sparked the most serious incident to date. It happened in the second quarter. The Bulldogs had just scored, running their lead to 23-14. The Lakers were bringing the ball back down the court, on the attack. Bobby moved out to the edge of his zone to meet the Laker dribbling toward him.

Suddenly Bobby leaped forward and speared the ball with his right hand. The Laker jerked back, but too late. Bobby's hand caught a part of the ball. It skittered across the floor. Bobby, with quickness and sure hands, got it. He stood free with the ball in his hands.

Skipper Denham, almost at the center stripe, was moving across the court toward the action. He stopped suddenly in his tracks when he saw Bobby had the ball. There was nothing between Skipper and the goal at the other end of the court.

"Run!" Bobby screamed at Skipper.

Skipper, startled by the command, stared blankly at Bobby for a split second. Then he turned and raced for the basket.

Bobby uncorked a baseball pass. He was aiming for the spot Skipper should have reached. But Skipper was not there. The split-second delay in his start proved fatal. The ball slithered off Skipper's outstretched fingers and bounced out-of-bounds.

Deke could see Bobby's lips moving. Bobby was shouting something at Skipper half the court away. The words were lost to Deke in the roar of the crowd brought to its feet by the fast turn of events. But Bobby's face told the story. Bobby, his face screwed into an ugly expression of anger, was spitting the words downcourt at Skipper. Then Bobby's expression changed from one of anger to one of undisguised contempt, and he turned his back on Skipper.

Skipper's lapse in getting started was unfortunate but understandable. Normally the Bulldogs played a deliberate style of attack. They set up their plays carefully. For a fraction of a second, Skipper had waited to set up a play. In this particular instance, it was a mistake. His own lack of speed kept him from making up for the mistake by racing under the baseball pass. But Bobby's outburst was unwarranted.

Clearly, Skipper heard the words Bobby had shouted at him. His face blanched as he returned to the court. The other players had heard Bobby, too.

Dennis said something to the shocked Skipper and received not even the slightest nod of acknowledgment in return. Ken Flaherty, jogging past Bobby on his way back to his defensive position, said something. His face was angry. Bobby turned on him with a snarl.

After the game, in the dressing room, Deke walked by Bobby and said quietly, "I want to see you in my office when you're dressed."

Bobby looked up, startled, and seemed ready to say something, but Deke kept walking.

When Bobby came to Deke's office, Deke got up from his desk, walked around and closed the door, telling Bobby, "Have a seat. This won't take a minute."

"Wow! This must be hot, closed door and all."

"Sit down," Deke repeated. "And wipe that grin off your face. I'm not in the mood for it."

The tone of Deke's voice and the uncharacteristic harshness of the remark seemed to stun Bobby for a minute. The cocky half smile vanished. Bobby sat himself down on a chair alongside Deke's desk.

Deke returned from closing the door and perched himself on the corner of his desk.

"That was inexcusable, that shouting of yours at Skipper," Deke said. He was looking Bobby in the eye. Bobby, expressionless, was returning the gaze. "Team members support each other. They don't criticize each other in the midst of a game. They don't ridicule each other. They don't embarrass each other."

"If that snob—"

"Cut it," Deke interrupted. "Cut it right there."

They stared at each other for half a minute without speaking.

"They all—"

"I'm not talking about what they all do," Deke said. "I'm talking about what you did. And I'm telling you that I will not stand for it. Nothing like that is ever to happen again. Do you understand?"

Bobby's eyes were angry. But all he said was, "Yes."

That had been a week ago last night, and nothing like it had happened again . . . yet.

Now, seated at his desk in his tiny office, Deke gave up on the game plan he was devising for the tough Warfield Tech Cardinals on Friday night, just two days away. He laid down his pencil and turned in his chair and stared out the window.

The season's first snow was falling. The big, wet

flakes were blowing in crazy swirls. This was going to be a heavy one. The stiff winds were going to pile up huge drifts.

Deke thought that nowhere do the wintry winds blow the way they do in the flat corn country of western Illinois. He loved it. This was home to him. He hoped that Bloomfield was going to be home, not just this year, but for many years to come. For that to be so, however, Deke knew that he was going to have to solve the problem of a widening chasm between the little redhead who was the leading scorer and the rest of the team. The problem was not going to solve itself. No doubt about that.

So far, except for the casual conversations with Benjy and Skipper, Deke had been content to move from victory to victory watching Bobby lead the team while he waged a cold war at the same time.

The snow outside the window was even heavier now. Deke wondered if the storm might force postponement of the Warfield Tech Cardinals' game here in Bloomfield. Such postponements were not rare in the course of a snowy Illinois winter. But it was only Wednesday. No matter how heavy the snow, the roads would be clear by Friday night.

The telephone on Deke's desk rang, interrupting his reverie. He turned in the chair and picked it up.

The voice of Wilfred Mulholland, the principal of Bloomfield High, came through on the line, crisp and firm as always. Could Deke drop by the principal's office this morning? And, yes, it involved "the Bobby Haggard problem."

"As you can understand, I've suspended the boy for three days," Wilfred Mulholland said. He was sitting behind his large, wooden desk, the office door closed, peering at Deke over glasses riding low on his nose. He wore a serious expression. "I had no choice."

Yes, Deke understood. And yes, Deke agreed that Mulholland had no choice.

The facts of the matter were simple, horribly simple: Bobby and one of the troublemakers he had linked up with, Phil Metzger, had set off firecrackers in a classroom. It was bad business. Shooting off firecrackers meant automatic suspension. Everyone knew it. There had been a rash of firecracker throwing in the corridors since school opened last September. It was a fad—take the dare, see if you can get away with it. The girls scream. The boys laugh. The guilty parties are heroes of a sort, at least in their own eyes. And they win a place at the center of attention. Mulholland had cracked down hard. A couple of weeks before, two students caught lighting firecrackers in the corridor had been suspended. Mulholland's tough disciplinary move had had the desired effect. There had been no recurrence until now.

Now Bobby and Phil Metzger had gone everybody one better. The weak of heart had faded from the field. Nobody was tossing firecrackers. So Bobby and Phil not only exploded firecrackers, they did so in a classroom. They were the greatest daredevils of all. They were sure to be caught and suspended.

Deke had not been surprised by the seriousness of the matter. From the moment of his brief telephone conversation with Mulholland, he had known there was real trouble ahead.

It wasn't that Mulholland referred to "the Bobby Haggard problem." Deke had heard the term before, and he was growing used to it. He had even heard the term from Mulholland before. The principal had used it when he called to advise Deke that Bobby was serving time in the early-morning punishment study hall for cutting a class. The cutting of one class did not affect Bobby's eligibility to play basketball, but more of it was sure to. On that occasion, the information from Mulholland was just that —information—and he had telephoned Deke.

But this time the principal had summoned Deke to his office. It was not Mulholland's style to deal with a serious matter on the telephone. Mulholland was an eye-to-eye man when it came to settling big problems. And he was calling Deke in for an eye-to-eye meeting.

Like so many of the high-school principals in the area, Mulholland had started his education career as a coach. Slender, stooped, with thinning gray hair, and glasses forever slipping down the bridge of his nose, he hardly looked the part. But thirty years ago he had been a good college basketball player. For ten years afterward he had been a dynamic coach developing outstanding teams. He was an innovative tactician and, so Deke had heard, a remarkable handler of the boys in his charge. The only lingering evidence of his background now was a habit of dropping in on the practice sessions occasionally. He never interfered or even offered coaching advice to Deke, but he always wore a wistful expression as he watched the players go through their paces, responding to Deke's instructions. Deke got the feeling the principal found pleasure in reliving, if only for a few moments, a good time in his life.

While Mulholland, speaking softly, almost sadly, had been describing the firecracker episode, Deke saw in his mind the cocky half grin on Bobby's face. The little red-head, the outsider, was showing them all. He was really dishing it out this time. He was getting even with every-body. He was taking center stage. As for the basketball team, well, they were sure to find out now that they needed him more than he needed them.

"I can appreciate the problems this creates for you,

with Warfield Tech coming up on Friday night," Mulholland said. He was watching Deke carefully.

True, the Warfield Tech Cardinals were sure to be the Bulldogs' toughest test of the season so far. Even with Bobby Haggard in the lineup, Warfield Tech presented a stiff challenge. Without Bobby, the Bulldogs were in trouble. Without Bobby's deadeye outside shooting, the Bulldogs would lose a lot of points. Beyond that, merely by lacking the threat of Bobby's shooting, the Bulldogs would invite the Cardinals to concentrate on guarding Benjy Holman and Skipper Denham. Without Bobby, the Bulldogs' attack was doomed to a sputtering uphill effort, a near hopeless assignment against the likes of the Warfield Tech Cardinals.

"There's more to it than this one game," Deke said. "This boy, Bobby Haggard, needs something, and I can't get a handle on it."

Mulholland nodded slightly. "You didn't know, did you?" he asked. "I mean, Bobby didn't tell you that he had been suspended before he left the building, did he?"

"No, he didn't," Deke said.

Deke felt a sense of failure. Mulholland, with his simple questions, had put the problem squarely into focus. Being a former coach, Mulholland recognized the essence of the problem. By this time, four weeks into the schedule, Deke should have won the confidence of all his players, Bobby Haggard included. They should all, Bobby and the rest of them, look to him, their coach, for guidance, advice, and understanding. Maybe the other players did. They had not been put to the test. But clearly Deke had not won over Bobby Haggard.

"No," Deke repeated, "he didn't tell me."

Mulholland seemed to read Deke's mind. "Don't feel guilty about it," he said.

Deke smiled weakly. He appreciated the principal's understanding of the dilemma. "There's got to be a solution out there somewhere," he said. "And I've got to find it—and quickly."

"Perhaps," Mulholland said, "this whole episode will turn out to be a blessing in disguise. After all, it does bring things to a head."

Deke reflected that the last time Bobby Haggard and his coach and his teammates came to a fork in the road, last year, everyone concerned took the wrong turn. The team was left in a shambles. The coach resigned in failure. And Bobby Haggard was left more an outsider than ever.

But Deke did not mention this to Mulholland. Instead, he said, "I hope you're right."

Deke walked from Mulholland's office through the empty corridors and past the filled classrooms, returning to his office.

Three days—Wednesday, Thursday, Friday. Deke had two days of practice, today and Thursday, to prepare his team for a game against Warfield Tech on Friday night without Bobby Haggard. And he had a very limited time to turn the disaster into a blessing—for Bobby Haggard, for the Bulldogs' basketball team, and for himself.

As Deke turned a corner and headed down the short flight of stairs leading to his office next to the gym, a bell rang. Behind him, students poured out of the classrooms and into the corridors. Deke took the last steps two at a time with his long legs and walked into his office. He tossed his sports jacket over the back of a chair and loosened his necktie.

Deke's desk was covered with the pieces of paper containing his notes and charts, the battle plan for the Bulldogs' game with Warfield Tech. With a shrug, Deke picked up the sheaf of papers and dumped them in the wastebasket.

"Back to the old drawing board," he said to himself. The plan was built around the skills of Bobby Haggard. But there wasn't going to be a Bobby Haggard on the court. Deke needed a new game plan. "I'll think of something," Deke mumbled.

"You're talking to yourself," came the voice of Arnie Hamilton from the door behind Deke.

Deke turned, startled. Arnie was smiling amiably. He was wearing a sweat shirt, as he always did when conducting the gym classes. The class had ended with the bell Deke had heard returning to his office.

Deke managed to return Arnie's smile. "I may be talking to myself more and more as time goes on," he said. "You know, in four years of college, they never once mentioned Bobby Haggard."

"The boys in the gym class were buzzing with stories about what happened," Arnie said. "What's up?"

Deke walked around his desk and settled into his chair, and Arnie stepped inside and leaned against the wall. Briefly Deke filled Arnie in on what Bobby had done and what Mulholland had dealt out for punishment.

Arnie's smile was gone. "That means Warfield Tech—"

"Yes," Deke said.

"And after that—"

"And after that, I don't know," Deke said. Already his imagination was conjuring up too many unpleasant scenarios. Bobby might never return to the team. The struggle to win him over, straighten him out, set him on the right course—the struggle might be over, already lost. Even if he did return, the wall between Bobby and his teammates would be higher and thicker, more impenetrable than ever. Bobby had let his teammates down. They would not forget.

"Have you spoken with Bobby?" Arnie asked.

"Not yet," Deke said.

10

It was noon when Deke, driving slowly on the snowy street, pulled to the curb in front of the small, white frame house where Bobby lived.

The snowstorm, after dumping a quick five inches, had left on the same high winds that brought it in. Only scattered flurries were falling as Deke stepped out of the car. The sky remained heavy and gray, holding a warning that more snow was coming.

The house needed a coat of paint. A garbage can, dented and rusty, stood in the snow at the corner of the small front yard. All across the flat yard, the limp and bent tops of grass and weeds broke through the blanket of snow, the dying evidence of a summer's neglect.

Above the door to the garage attached to the side of the house, a basketball backboard stood with its netless hoop protruding. The sight was not unusual in Bloomfield and the surrounding towns of western Illinois. Every house, it seemed, had its backboard and hoop. The neighborhood backboards were the making of the legendary players and the outstanding teams of the area. Deke found it easy to imagine the number of times that Bobby Haggard, standing on the driveway, had squinted at the hoop and let fly with a shot. Probably a million times, Deke thought. He himself had fired a million shots—or so it seemed—at the hoop over his own garage door.

Deke walked around his car and picked his way carefully on the snow-slick sidewalk toward the porch.

As he glanced at the house, Deke wondered how much of the problem of Bobby Haggard might be explained by the dreary proof that nobody cared. Deke never had met either of Bobby's parents. If they ever came to see their son play, Deke was not aware of it. Bobby's father, as best Deke could learn, drifted from one job to another, and his mother worked as a check-out clerk at a supermarket. Wilfred Mulholland's secretary had had a difficult time tracking her down to notify her of Bobby's suspension. She had seemed concerned, true enough, but she had seemed more worried about being called to the telephone while at work. To Deke, the unkempt house said a lot. The peeling paint, the weeds, the rusty garbage can abandoned in the snow did not spell poverty so much as indifference. The signs were clear. And inside the house, a boy bore his own signs of nobody caring.

Bobby's teammates on the Bulldogs' basketball team were a constant reminder of his plight. Benjy Holman lived in a large and beautifully manicured home on the edge of town. His father, a physician, was a community leader. His parents never missed a Bulldog game, at home or on the road. The other players, while coming from families less prosperous than Benjy's, enjoyed the same support from their parents. They were going through life knowing they *belonged*. Bobby Haggard was going through life an outsider—at home, on the basketball team, everywhere.

Deke felt he was able to understand. His own family, while loving and caring, was not wealthy. They were far from being the social leaders of the town. As a boy, Deke was able to see the difference. He sensed the gap between himself and those who rode in big cars, lived in big houses, and had fathers who ran the town. With them, he had felt himself an outsider, with or without good reason.

But Deke did not, as he viewed himself while a boy in high school or as a coach dealing with Bobby Haggard today, see the solution in breaking the rules and rejecting the world. Instead, Deke had found basketball to be his route to a success overriding all his doubts. So, too, must Bobby Haggard.

"Seems I'm pretty good at defining the problem, but I'm not having much luck at finding the solution," he said to himself, as he pressed the buzzer at the front door.

Bobby opened the door. "Oh, it's you," he said.

For a brief moment, Deke thought he detected a new ingredient in Bobby's expression. His face seemed shaded, if only slightly, by remorse and disappointment. To Deke, it was a hopeful sign. Never before had he seen Bobby express the slightest hint of doubt or regret. Deke had the feeling he was getting a glimpse of the Bobby Haggard who was hiding behind the defensive wall. Bobby had sneered when he stole the ball from Dennis North in practice. He had snarled when Skipper Denham failed to get downcourt for a pass. That was the Bobby Haggard Deke knew, always attacking. But perhaps Bobby knew now that he had gone over the bounds in his classroom behavior. This was trouble he did not want. He had had a couple of hours alone to think it over.

Even before Deke could speak, however, Bobby's expression snapped back into the familiar cocky half grin, with defiance glistening in his brown eyes.

"We need to talk," Deke said.

"Okay," Bobby said. But he made no move to invite Deke into the house.

"It'll get cold in there if we leave the door open like this while we talk," Deke said. He forced a smile with his words.

Bobby shrugged and stepped back. Deke walked through the door into a plainly furnished, slightly shabby living room.

"Is your mother home?"

"No, she's working."

"Oh."

"You need to see her?" Bobby asked suddenly. His

eyes seemed to be sending forth a challenge. "Is that what you're here for?"

"Nope," Deke said casually, dropping his topcoat on the sofa and sitting down beside it. "Your mother does not play on the Bulldogs' basketball team. You do. It's you I came to talk to."

Bobby perched himself on the arm of an overstuffed chair and leaned back.

Deke studied Bobby's face. The grin was frozen in place. The eyes were darting from side to side, meeting Deke's gaze and then shifting suddenly away, then back.

"I'll get right to the point," Deke said. "I have some bad news for you."

"Oh?" Bobby said. Bobby's exaggerated air of indifference gave him away. Bobby was expecting Deke to announce his expulsion from the team—for good—and he was ready to demonstrate that it didn't matter.

"No," Deke said, waving a hand, "I'm not throwing you off the team."

Bobby looked a bit startled, as if suddenly aware that his innermost thoughts were being spoken aloud.

"I would not need to drive over here on this snowy day to notify you that you're no longer a member of the team," Deke said, intentionally going back on his promise to get right to the point. "I could have called you on the telephone, or I could have just waited to see if you tried to come back."

Bobby was watching Deke closely.

"Throwing you off the team would be the easy way—for you, and for me," Deke said. "You deserve to be bounced off the team, no doubt about it. You've let the team down by your stupid, childish misbehavior. The Bulldogs probably are going to lose an important game on Friday night because of what you've done. I don't think we can possibly win against Warfield Tech with one of our starters missing."

"Did you come here to—"

"No," Deke interrupted.

Bobby squirmed slightly in his perch on the arm of the chair. Clearly, he was wishing the conversation would come to an end.

"Hear me out," Deke said.

Deke waited until Bobby nodded slightly. "If we lose the game, and I think we will, you are going to find your own dumb antics catching all the blame. Your teammates are going to blame you for it. Your fellow students are going to blame you for it. The fans in this town are going to blame you for it. And, frankly, I am going to blame you for it, too."

Bobby opened his mouth as if to speak. But Deke waved him into silence.

"I know that you were going to say that you don't care. God knows, you have gone out of your way since the first day we met to prove to me that you don't care. You've been able to get away with it. But now things are different. You've got a problem. You've got a tough decision to make."

"What. . . ?"

"First of all, if you don't come back to the team after your suspension, everyone is going to say that you simply didn't have the guts to face up to the people you let down—your teammates, your school, your town, and, yes, your coach. And you will never again have a chance to prove them wrong. If your decision is to quit—well, that's part of the bad news I mentioned, and you're going to have to face it."

Deke paused. He wanted his point to sink in. Bobby had quit last year when Clair Thornton benched him. It was almost a hero's exit—or, at least, Bobby was able to see it that way. This time it was different.

"But coming back to the team may be even tougher," Deke said, leaning forward. "You're going to meet with —well, the only word for it is resentment. Your teammates are going to resent what you've done. Your schoolmates are going to resent it. All the fans in Bloomfield are going to resent it. And, yes, I'll tell you that I'm going to resent it, too.

"You're going to have one hell of a tough time, and you may as well know it. You may not have the guts for it. I don't know. But you should understand that you are going to have to be one hell of a man to win your way back. You are going to have to be a different Bobby Haggard—and you know exactly what I mean—to succeed."

Bobby stared at Deke without speaking. His face was blank. There was neither the defiant glare nor the cocky half grin.

"That's what I meant by bad news, Bobby," Deke said. "You have no easy way out. Whether you quit, or whether you come back, you're in for a tough time—tougher than you're going to want, believe me. You've made yourself a dilemma, created it by your own stupidity."

Deke felt his heart pounding in the silence of the small room. He tried to read some meaning in Bobby's blank expression. Perhaps he had been too tough, too harsh. For a moment he considered adding a word of advice—come back to the team, change your ways, face the music, and win in the end—but decided against it. If Deke understood what made Bobby tick, Bobby would make the right move. Advice right now might make the right move more difficult. But Deke knew, too, that if he had misread Bobby, this was the end.

"That's all I have to say, Bobby," Deke said with an easy air he did not feel at all. He got to his feet and picked up his topcoat from the sofa. "I wanted you to know the way I see it in no uncertain terms. So you can make your decision."

Deke walked out the door, leaving Bobby seated on the arm of the overstuffed chair.

11

"I must be crazy," Deke Warden said to himself.

He was standing at the sideline, watching his Bulldogs and the Warfield Tech Cardinals complete their warm-up shots. The Bloomfield High gym was packed, as usual, for the game. The band was blaring. The crowd was chattering. Punctuating the noise was the thumping sound of basketball hitting wood. All the sounds blended into a familiar symphony that always gave Deke a thrill. The powerful arc lights were bathing the playing court. The green-clad Bulldogs were running through a lay-up drill under the basket to Deke's left. The Cardinals in their white uniforms with red trim were taking their shots at the basket to Deke's right. The opening tip-off was only minutes away.

Crazy was the word, all right, Deke reflected, but in the last two days Deke had felt his hopes rising. There was, he was convinced, a chance that his Bulldogs were going to be able to whip Warfield Tech even without Bobby Haggard.

Every consideration indicated the Bulldogs were heading for a humiliating defeat. One of their starters was sidelined, which hurts any team. For the Bulldogs, the missing starter happened to be the leading scorer, the best dribbler, and a top defensive player. The loss was serious. And opposite the Bulldogs were the Warfield Tech Cardinals. They were unquestionably the best team on the Bulldogs' schedule so far. The Cardinals, with only one loss in seven games, were a formidable test for anyone. Deke, glancing at them in their warm-up drills, was impressed. He thought ruefully that they looked every bit as good as their record. The Cardinals' slender little black player reminded Deke of Bobby Haggard. He dribbled smoothly and easily, and he pumped in high, arching shots from the outside. He was going to be hard to stop. The big fellow at center was sure to give Benjy Holman a tough battle under the basket. Appearances suggested the Bulldogs did not have a chance with Bobby Haggard missing from the lineup.

But starting with a brief team meeting on Wednesday afternoon, Deke saw signs of hope. The first tiny glimmers grew into full-blown optimism as the two days passed leading up to the game.

Only three hours after Deke told Bobby Haggard that

the Bulldogs were going to lose, the players trooped into the locker room to dress for practice. Deke eyed them as they came in and began changing from their classroom clothes into their practice uniforms. By this time, they all knew Bobby had been suspended. The corridor grapevine had carried the report as swiftly as ever. The players knew that Bobby was out of the Warfield Tech game and perhaps gone for the season.

"Before we go onto the court for practice," Deke said, "let's clear the air of something."

The players turned to him. Nobody appeared to be surprised. They knew what was coming. They were expecting it.

Deke closed the locker-room door and stepped into the center of the floor.

"You already know, I suppose, that Bobby has been suspended for three days. That means he will be missing the Warfield Tech game. It's a tough blow for us. Warfield Tech is a good team. You know their record. We were facing a real battle even at full strength. It's going to be tougher with one of our starters missing from the lineup." Deke paused and looked around at the serious faces surrounding him. "We've got to change our plans for the game, and we've got only today and tomorrow to do it. That means a lot of hard work and concentration. I know that each of you will be putting out your best—the extra effort. That's what it's going to take."

Deke carefully avoided promising a victory for a Bulldog team lacking the outside shooting of Bobby Haggard. The players knew what was missing. They understood the odds.

And Deke intentionally omitted any reference to the question of whether Bobby Haggard ever would be back with the Bulldogs. Deke did not know the answer to that one himself.

Deke turned to open the locker-room door and send the players out to practice, but Skipper Denham's voice stopped him.

"Coach, we'll win without him," Skipper said. He spoke the words in a flat, conversational tone, simply stating what he saw as a fact.

"Who needs the dude?" Benjy chimed in. His face was expressionless, his brown eyes unblinking. "I'm sick of hearing that we're nothing without him."

Deke looked at the unsmiling faces around him. The locker room was deathly quiet. For a brief moment, Deke felt a pang of guilt for not telling them himself that they were able to win without the little redhead with the arrogant grin. Deke had not, until this moment, thought there was a chance. Any prediction he might make of victory without Bobby Haggard was bound to sound hollow. He was certain to come across as phony, simply saying what the coach was expected to say, nothing more. But coming from a player it was different. Skipper's announcement carried more weight than any statement Deke could have made.

Deke smiled. "I think that is exactly what we should do—win without him," Deke said.

The players moved through the practice session with an air of determination that heightened Deke's hopes another notch. They were not a laughing bunch, for sure. They were working, and working hard.

Deke's revised game plan was simple. They were going to have to do without Bobby's outside shooting. Neither Dennis North at one of the guard positions nor Chris Santini, subbing for Bobby at the other guard slot, possessed the good shooting eye for the long pumper. They offered nothing even close to Bobby's consistency from the outside. So Deke switched the hub of the attack to Skipper's reliable push shots from the corner. Deke was counting on Skipper to provide enough of a threat to pull some of the Cardinals' defense off Benjy under the basket.

Deke was almost smiling when he sent the players to the showers at the close of the drills. It had been a good practice.

In his office, Deke found three telephone messages on his desk: Herbie Foxx wanted to speak to him; so did the sports director of a Peoria television station and the sports editor of the Peoria newspaper.

The word was out, of course, that the sparkplug of the undefeated Bloomfield Bulldogs had been suspended from school. Bobby Haggard was going to be missing the Bulldogs' game with the tough Warfield Tech Cardinals. Some comment from the coach was needed, and they were calling for it.

Deke leaned back in his desk chair and stared at the messages for a moment, framing his words in his mind, and then he leaned forward and picked up the telephone.

He placed the two Peoria calls ahead of the one to Herbie Foxx. The sports director of the television station and the sports editor of the paper both were sympathetic. Deke had known them since his earliest playing days at

Illinois State. He always got along well with them. They settled for Deke's brief, simple statement: an accounting of what had happened, an admission that losing Bobby Haggard hurt the Bulldogs, and a refusal to guess the outcome of the Warfield Tech game.

"Now for Herbie Foxx." Deke sighed. He glanced at his watch. The time was five thirty. Herbie was sure to be getting frantic. His six o'clock sports show was right around the corner. Deke dreaded talking to him.

Herbie had hopped on the bandwagon early in the Bulldogs' winning streak. To be sure, Deke wanted his support. Herbie's evening radio show and his play-by-play game descriptions carried enormous influence in Bloomfield. More important, the players themselves listened to Herbie's commentaries. They heard, too, from their friends what Herbie was saying about them in his play-by-play broadcasts of the games. The players had grown up listening to Herbie Foxx. Herbie was, beyond a doubt, important to Deke's success as Bulldogs' basketball coach.

But Herbie's on-the-air support had turned out to be a mixed blessing. For one thing, his overly exuberant optimism about the revitalized Bulldogs made Deke cringe. Herbie was sprinkling his broadcasts with forecasts of an undefeated season, a state championship, records of all sorts. Deke saw all too easily the dangers of building up hopes high as the sky. The higher the hopes, the bigger the letdown. Deke had tried to talk to Herbie about it. "Just keep rolling," Herbie had said, refusing to admit he might be causing a problem.

Without ever saying so, Herbie seemed to be taking

credit for the Bulldogs' winning ways. He succeeded in getting across the message that every one of Bobby Haggard's field goals was just renewed vindication of Herbie's slashing campaign to rid Bloomfield of Clair Thornton as coach.

Deke knew, too, that Herbie's support could be lost as quickly as it was won. Herbie had been quick to take up the cheers when the Bulldogs came out of the starting gate a winner, and he forgot about his early antagonism toward Deke. But Herbie was capable of flip-flopping back to a vote of no confidence, and doing so just as quickly. The sidelining of Bobby Haggard, although Deke was not the cause, could very easily trigger Herbie's flip-flop.

"Just heard about Bobby a few minutes ago," Herbie barked into the telephone. "Why didn't you call me when it happened?"

"I had a lot of other things on my mind at the moment, Herbie."

"This is bad," Herbie snapped.

Deke paused a moment. Bad for whom? Bad for the team, or for Bobby, or for Deke, or for Herbie himself, who loved a winner and detested a loser? Deke cautioned himself against being pulled into an overstatement by Herbie's pushy manner. Then he said, "We will certainly miss Bobby. You know that as well as I do, Herbie. The whole episode was unfortunate. We'll be ready for Warfield Tech. But for sure, no team can lose one of its better players without feeling the results."

"What do you mean—one of the *better* players? He's the whole team."

Deke measured his words carefully. "Bobby Haggard has been important—mighty important—to the Bulldogs. I'll grant you that. But I do not agree that any one player is the whole team."

Herbie harrumphed, and Deke wished that he had, in the course of the hectic day, found a moment to call Herbie. He had missed a chance to make a tactical gain with the broadcaster.

"I'll tell you one thing that you'd better remember," Herbie said, "and that's that we got rid of the coach last year who was unable, for whatever reasons, to capitalize on Bobby Haggard's talents."

Deke felt his temper flare. But he said nothing.

"This town is lucky to have a player of Bobby Haggard's caliber," Herbie continued, "and the coach's job is to make sure that he's playing."

"No comment, Herbie," Deke said icily.

"That's okay," Herbie fired back. "I'll do the commenting for both of us."

And, indeed, Herbie did.

Deke, having showered and dressed, was driving from the school to his apartment when Herbie's nightly sports show came on the air. Deke started to turn off his car radio. He could imagine what Herbie was going to say. But instead of turning the radio off, Deke turned up the volume. The fans, not to mention his players, were sure to be listening all over Bloomfield. Like it or not, Deke needed to know what was being said.

"The Warfield Tech game is shaping up as a real nostalgia trip for the Bloomfield High fans," Herbie announced in his staccato style. "If you're longing for a return to the old days—remember all those defeats last year?—you're going to get your chance for a sentimental journey into the past on Friday night. And why's that? Well, folks, the Bulldogs are right back where they were last year. That's right, Bobby Haggard is not in the lineup."

Pulling to the curb in front of his apartment, Deke let the engine idle to listen to the remainder of Herbie's commentary. He could not help seeing in his mind the serious faces of Benjy and Skipper and all the others listening to Herbie's biting sarcasm. Deke could imagine the feelings of Chris, trying to step into Bobby's shoes. And Deke also wondered if Bobby was listening. Was Bobby wearing the cocky half smile?

"We changed coaches, you'll remember, after the disaster of last year," Herbie was saying. "The Bulldogs were lacking leadership in the coaching job. We were all saying it. So we changed coaches. For a while it looked like everything was working. We had a new coach. We had Bobby Haggard in there scoring more than twenty points a game. And we were winning. But now it's like it was all a mirage. It looks like we're the same old Bulldogs—a new face for a coach, but the same old problems. It looks like we're in for a rerun of last year. If you don't believe me, folks, just drop by the gym on Friday night and watch the Bulldogs get trounced."

Angrily Deke turned off the radio and got out of the car.

The telephone was ringing when Deke unlocked his front door and stepped into his apartment. He picked up the instrument without stopping to take off his coat.

"Did you hear that?" The voice was Skipper's. The anger fairly sparkled over the telephone line with each word. Skipper did not bother to explain what he was asking about.

"Yes, I heard it," Deke said.

"I'm going to call all the players, tell 'em it doesn't matter what Herbie Foxx says."

"All right," Deke said. "I think that's a good idea."

"We are going to win on Friday night," Skipper said and hung up.

So in the end Herbie's outburst helped raise Deke's hopes about his Bulldogs' chances against Warfield Tech.

Crazy, Deke thought again. Nobody loses their leading scorer and still is able to whip a team like this Warfield Tech outfit. Crazy, for sure. But crazy things work sometimes.

The players were approaching the bench now for the final moment before the game-opening tip-off.

The referee was walking toward the center of the court with the ball under his arm.

Deke knelt into the circle of players. They clasped hands.

"Now is the time to do it," Deke said, and he sent them onto the court.

12

But the Bulldogs did not defeat Warfield Tech. They were going to win the game without Bobby Haggard, but they were not able to do it.

Neither Deke Warden nor his players accepted the fact of defeat until the waning seconds of the game. And in the end the loss was no one's fault. No one, that is, except the Warfield Tech Cardinals, who refused to buckle in the face of the Bulldogs' inspired play, and Bobby Haggard, who was absent from the Bulldogs' lineup.

Skipper Denham did his job for the Bulldogs in the corner. Always serious, Skipper's face showed more than usual concentration and determination. Deke had the feeling that the gym could have burned down around Skipper and he would not have noticed, so intent was he on every pass, every dribble, every shot. He established himself early as a scoring threat from the corner. The lure worked. The Cardinals had to shift their defense slightly to meet Skipper's offense. The shift eased the burden on Benjy Holman under the basket. Despite the added pressure he drew upon himself, Skipper finished the game with eighteen points, his high point-production of the season.

Benjy, battling hard against Warfield Tech's large, muscular, and skilled center, got sixteen points and grabbed twelve rebounds. Considering the ability of his opponent under the basket, the game undoubtedly was the best of Benjy's career so far.

The others, too, played to the full limit of their abilities, and then some—Ken Flaherty, Dennis North, Chris Santini.

The Bulldogs' superior effort was evident from the start.

The Cardinals were loose and easy in the opening minute. Deke sensed they were a bit overconfident, knowing that one of the Bulldogs' important starters was missing from the lineup, but they realized quickly they were going against a team determined to win, no matter the odds. And the Cardinals settled into the struggle with faces every bit as grim as the Bulldogs'.

Even the Bulldogs' fans, usually a thunderous bunch keeping up a steady stream of roaring cheers, sat in a strange, almost reverent silence. There was no reason to sing out their favorite chant, "Go-Bobby-Go! Go-Bobby-Go!" They knew Bobby wasn't there, and they knew why. They had heard Herbie Foxx's broadcast, too. But to Deke their silence seemed less a lack of support than a matter of joining the players in the intense effort to win without Bobby. It was as if they, by contributing their own concentration, might help the Bulldogs pull off the impossible.

The Bulldogs delivered a remarkable effort. Deke felt his admiration for the boys on the court grow with every play. Once, in the third quarter, his eyes met Benjy's as the tall center ran down the court after a field goal. At that point they both knew, without exchanging a word, that only a miracle could bring the Bulldogs home a winner. But neither of them was ready to admit it. The look in Benjy's eyes gave Deke a lump in his throat. Deke wished he could take the court himself. The Bulldogs needed him. They deserved to win.

But at the final buzzer the scoreboard read: Bulldogs 59, Visitors 66.

Warfield Tech had led all the way.

From the start, the Cardinals took advantage of Bobby Haggard's absence. Deke was not the only coach who went back to the drawing board to change his game plan because of Bobby's suspension. Obviously, the Warfield Tech coach had revised his strategy. He knew of Bobby's suspension. He knew there was an unexpected chink in the Bulldogs' armor. He was going to take advantage of it. He was going to cash in on it.

The Cardinals clamped a full-court press on the Bulldogs from the opening minute. Their guards stayed downcourt and harassed Ken Flaherty and Chris Santini trying to bring the ball up the court. The guards had the speed for the job. The Warfield Tech forwards, too, were quick enough to make the strategy pay off. They were able to cover their end of the court against the threat of a long pass. The full-court press was a smart move for the Cardinals, with the Bulldogs' best dribbler and ball handler missing. The Cardinals might rattle a less expert substitute. And they did. They might steal the ball for an important field goal. And they did. They might force fumbles, and they might intercept uncertain and hasty passes. And they did. Ken and Chris fought hard, never giving up, but they were no match for the Cardinals' full-court press.

On defense, too, the Bulldogs missed Bobby. The Cardinals collected on Bobby's absence. The little Warfield Tech guard, the slender, quick black player who reminded Deke of Bobby, pumped in thirty-one points. He dribbled around and past Ken and Chris. He got his rapid-fire shots away without effective harassment. Deke watched in admiration. The boy was a copy of Bobby Haggard. And only Bobby Haggard's quick hands and feet might have stuck with him and controlled him. Without Bobby in the Bulldogs' lineup, the guard ran wild.

Walking off the court at the end of the game, Deke looked back at the final score in lights: 66-59, a defeat. Eight points away from victory.

Bobby Haggard, with his twenty-point scoring average, would have made the difference on offense alone. He would have made the difference on defense, too, surely depriving the hot-shooting black guard of at least eight of his points. Clearly, Bobby Haggard—or, more precisely, the absence of Bobby Haggard—was the difference, and the fact was inescapable.

The thought troubled Deke as he walked to the dressing room. He knew the same thoughts were in the minds of his players. They did not like Bobby Haggard. They never had. They had been told by everyone—their friends, the townspeople, the staccato voice of Herbie Foxx—that victory depended on Bobby Haggard. The assumption was not easy to swallow. And now, tonight, they had been determined to show the world and themselves that it was not true, that they could, indeed, win without Bobby Haggard. They were going to do it. But they could not. The Bulldogs needed Bobby to win the big one. The fact was not pleasant. None of the players were going to like Bobby Haggard the more for it.

And what about Bobby himself?

Deke decided that question would have to wait for an answer, and he managed to wipe the deep frown off his face as he pushed through the dressing-room door.

The dressing room was deathly quiet. None of the players had gone to the showers yet. They were sitting, slumped, on the benches in front of the lockers. Some of them were toweling off the perspiration slowly, easily, trying to relax. The five starters, who had played almost the entire game without relief, were still breathing heavily. They were an exhausted bunch. They had put in a furious thirty-two minutes of basketball. The physical effort had been enormous. But in addition to the strain of running, jumping, passing, and shooting, they had paid a high price in mental effort. Deke knew full well the exhausting effects of tension alone in a tough and important game. Losing took its toll, too. In place of the exhilaration of winning, there was the depression of defeat. The physical exhaustion seemed without purpose in the doldrums of defeat. For the Bulldogs, also, there was an added ingredient. This game was not just a loss to be marked up and laid away with the record books. Until tonight, the Bulldogs were an undefeated team. An undefeated record is borne proudly. It vanishes with one loss, and the taste is bitter. All the more bitter, to be sure, when the victory string is broken because of the absence of a player nobody liked.

Deke thought at first that he could not imagine a team with more reasons for feeling down in the dumps. A loss is bad enough. The end of a victory string is even worse. Attributing the loss to Bobby Haggard simply served to pour salt in the wound. All of the reasons together created an almost visible cloud of gloom throughout the dressing room.

When Deke stepped in and closed the door behind him, he did not know what to say. Then, without thought, he spoke. The words seemed natural to him.

"Smile, dammit," he barked. With some effort, he put down his own disappointment and spread a grin across his face.

The players, startled, looked at him. They did not believe the words. They did not believe the smile they saw on his face. The expressions of shock changed into blank stares of puzzlement.

"You played a great game—all of you—and I'm

proud of you," Deke said. "You lost. Nobody likes losing. You don't, and I don't. But if I coach for a hundred years, I will never be prouder of a team than I am tonight. You were great. You played a winner's game—tough and smart and never letting up, never giving up. You were beautiful, and I love you. Hold up your heads. You're entitled."

None of the Bulldog players smiled. Nobody even nodded.

Deke understood. He did not feel like smiling either.

The players were gone and the gym was empty when Deke came out of the dressing room and walked alongside the court toward the lobby door.

Deke's smile, put on for the benefit of the players, had long since faded. The deep frown was back in place. He knew that the players were going to recover from the disappointment of the defeat. Deke was going to recover, too. But now, with the consuming excitement of the game behind him, Deke's mind moved back to the unanswered question: what about Bobby Haggard?

The loss undoubtedly would make Bobby less welcome than ever in the eyes of his teammates. The little redhead's face was going to be a reminder to every last one of them that they lost without him, lost because of him. Bobby's wisecracking remarks, his sharp needling, his messages of contempt sparkling out of his eyes, everything was going to grate on the players more than ever. Tempers, already quicker than Deke wanted, were going to fray more rapidly than before. Even if Bobby kept a straight face and a closed mouth, none of the players would find any joy in the sight of him. His mere presence was bound to stir trouble.

That is, if—and the word loomed large in Deke's mind—if Bobby returned to the team. He might not. Deke knew his quitting was a real possibility. Bobby had quit last year. The circumstances this time were different. But Bobby surely knew what he faced in trying to return to the team. Deke had laid out the facts for him. Every one of Deke's warning words took on added weight now, in the wake of the defeat. Bobby was smart enough to know it. He might decide that basketball, his greatest hope of becoming an insider instead of an outsider, was not worth the struggle and the discipline. If he did, Deke knew that he, the coach, would have failed. Somehow, he thought to himself, the game scores, the victories and defeats, did not seem to matter as much.

Deke was still frowning as he shoved open the door of the gym and stepped into the lobby. A few fans remained. They were waiting inside, sheltered from the wintry night, for the traffic to clear before going to their cars. Deke could see the lights of the cars creeping along on the street in front of the gym.

"A tough one to lose," one of the fans said.

"Sure was," Deke replied. He smiled wanly but kept moving, not wishing to get caught in a discussion of the game.

"Would have been different with Bobby in there, huh?" another fan said.

"Sure would've," Deke said.

He pushed open the front door and stepped out. The

cold winter wind on the field-house porch caused him to shiver. Deke stopped to fold over the flap of his coat and button the top button before walking around the building to his parking spot on the side. Several small knots of people were standing on the porch, keeping an eye on the slow procession of cars in the street, watching for their rides home.

Off to his left, Deke spotted Bobby Haggard. Bobby was alone. Instinctively Deke glanced around for the boys Bobby ran with, Phil Metzger and Bill Hainey. Deke was not able to recognize everyone in the darkness of the field-house porch, but Bobby's usual friends appeared to be nowhere in the area.

"I hear that we lost," Bobby said.

"Didn't you see it?"

"No, I just—"

"We sure could have used you out there tonight," Deke said quickly.

Bobby did not answer. For an instant there was a trace of the cocky half grin. Then it disappeared. "I've been thinking," he said finally.

"Yes?"

"I'll be at practice on Monday."

"Good," Deke said.

13

Deke Warden was grateful for the weekend.

His players needed the Saturday and Sunday holiday from school. They needed the brief respite from basketball. The loss to Warfield Tech had been a tough one. The Bulldogs saw their victory string snapped. They no longer were an undefeated team. They had the unpleasant fact that, yes, they did need Bobby Haggard proven to them. Even the closeness of the final score was, in a way, demoralizing. Only eight points away from victory. The starting five were bound to be replaying the game in their minds—shots they missed, points they allowed an opponent to make. A small difference here, a small difference there, and they might have won. The remembering was not going to be enjoyable. No, this would not be a happy weekend for his players, Deke was sure. But he was equally certain the weekend would be useful to them.

As for Deke, he resolved to break one of his own basic rules for sound basketball coaching. He decided to look ahead one game in his planning. The Bulldogs' next opponent, Adamsville East on Tuesday night, should be a breather. The Wolverines were having a bad year. They had won only two games and, on paper, did not have a chance of challenging the Bulldogs. But looming just three days beyond Adamsville East were the mighty Mount Perry Tigers, coming to Bloomfield on Friday night. Deke decided to let the Adamsville East game take care of itself. No special strategy was needed to handle it. He was going to concentrate on plans for the Mount Perry Tigers.

Treating an opponent lightly was risky business, and Deke knew it. The history of basketball is filled with instances of hapless teams rising up and knocking off a high-riding, heavily favored powerhouse. The danger is greatest in high school, where the players are less experienced, less polished, and less consistent than in college.

But Deke made up his mind to take the chance after hearing the one short sentence from Bobby Haggard on the field-house porch: "I'll be at practice on Monday."

With Bobby playing, and the Bulldogs at full strength, the Adamsville East Wolverines were no match. They were no problem at all. Deke was sure of it. He was just being realistic.

Bobby's statement cast the Mount Perry game in a different light, too. With Bobby in the lineup, the Bulldogs had a chance—but only a chance, nothing more—of whipping the Tigers. Without Bobby pumping in the shots from the outside, the Bulldogs were dead. But the Bulldogs were going to have him, and they had a chance to win.

The burden now rested with Deke. As the coach, he had to find the secret of victory. He was the one who must discover how to turn the chance of it into the reality. He must provide the edge, however slight, that spells victory. In close games, the team with the better coach almost always comes out the winner. A smart coach, well prepared, provides the crucial point or two of difference that wins the close games.

The Bloomfield fans, too, were looking past the easy Adamsville East game and aiming for the exciting prospect of defeating mighty Mount Perry.

Even before Deke left his apartment on Saturday morning, the telephone rang and the voice of Herbie Foxx snapped the question, "Bobby Haggard is coming back to the team, isn't he? We'll have him for the Mount Perry game, won't we?"

"I'm assuming so," Deke replied, deciding there was no need to tell Herbie about the conversation with Bobby on the field-house porch. "It was just a three-day suspension."

"We're going to need him against Mount Perry," Herbie stated. "No chance without him." There was a pause, and then Herbie added, speaking in a softened tone Deke never had heard out of him, "The boys played well against Warfield Tech without Bobby. Too bad they couldn't pull it out."

"I was proud of them," Deke said, "and I told them so in the dressing room. They were pretty down in the dumps."

Downtown, everywhere that Deke went—the laundry, the supermarket for his week's groceries, the drugstore for toiletries, and at Nemo's Café for lunch—the talk was the same. Will Bobby Haggard be back for the Mount Perry game? Tough luck against Warfield Tech. And, how about Mount Perry, anyway? They're going to be tough.

Tough was hardly the word. The runner-up team in the state championship tournament last year, the Mount Perry Tigers were every bit as strong this year, maybe even stronger. They were tall, fast, and skilled. They had marched past their first eight opponents without a loss or even a serious threat of a loss. Their victories were impressive. Not a single one of their opponents had come within ten points of the awesome Tigers. Last year they lost the state championship by a whisker. This year, well, they were going to win it. That was what everyone was saying. The evidence was piling up with each new victory.

But Deke knew that if everything—*everything*—was right, then the Bulldogs would topple Mount Perry.

Deke kept counting in his mind the reasons he wanted to defeat Mount Perry. Any victory is sweet. A victory feels better than a loss. Beating Mount Perry, of course, would be the sweetest of all victories. Beyond that, Deke saw the deeper meanings of a triumph over Mount Perry. Victory would mean that his Bulldogs were a team, a whole unit, for the first time. They could win with nothing less. Victory would mean that "the Bobby Haggard problem" was solved. Personally, Deke knew that victory would mean that he was smart enough as a coach to find the winning ingredients in a close game. And, looking ahead, Deke was sure the Mount Perry game was going to be the season's turning point for his Bulldogs. Victory would provide the impetus for a fabulously successful season.

So, on Sunday, Deke drove to a television station at Peoria to view the videotape of the Tigers' losing effort in last year's state championship game. Few of the teams in this area of small towns scattered through western Illinois ever had their games televised. Only those who won their way into the state tournament wound up on videotape. Mount Perry happened to be one, and Deke was determined to pursue any opportunity to learn more about the Tigers. The smallest tidbit of information might provide the key to the winning point.

The sports director of the television station readily agreed to cooperate, as Deke had known he would. The sports director had handled the play-by-play broadcasts of the Illinois State games. He and Deke had been on a friendly, first-name basis since Deke's freshman days at Illinois State.

Even the Mount Perry coach cooperated. "No objections," Bernard MacKay said with a laugh, when Deke called as a courtesy gesture to say he planned to look at the videotape. MacKay seemed amused by the thought that Deke actually was entertaining hopes of winning. "But remember," MacKay said, "we lost that championship game, and we're not planning to lose again for a while."

MacKay's remark surprised Deke and, in a way, encouraged him. Coaches seldom voiced such confidence, and for good reason. An undefeated team needed to fight against overconfidence. But here was MacKay, a veteran coach, sounding so confident, almost patronizing. Perhaps MacKay was assuming the Bulldogs were not going to have Bobby Haggard back in the lineup. He surely knew that Bobby had departed in mid-season last year after rumblings of trouble. He surely knew that Bobby had missed the Warfield Tech game because of a suspension. Perhaps MacKay concluded history was repeating itself, and Bobby Haggard was gone for good.

Either way Deke came away from the telephone conversation with MacKay suspecting he might have found one weakness in the Mount Perry Tigers, overconfidence, before he even looked at the first moment of the videotape.

The videotape was worth the trip to Deke. Although two of the Tigers' starters from last year's team had graduated, the film offered Deke a rich lode of valuable information. The Tigers' style of play was bound to be the same this year. They had the same coach and, for the most part, the same players.

As for the individuals on the Mount Perry team, Deke got a chance to see them all. Even the boys who this year were replacing the graduating seniors from last year's team appeared in the game as substitutes. They put in enough playing time to give Deke a good look.

By late afternoon, Deke had filled most of the pages of a notebook. He jotted down weaknesses he spotted. He noted the strengths he was going to have to find a way to nullify or reduce. He wrote down the ideas that popped into his mind as he watched.

Having watched the videotape and then having re-watched it, Deke felt he knew the Mount Perry Tigers as well as he knew his own Bulldogs.

The thought gave Deke pause. With Bobby Haggard coming back in the wake of the Warfield Tech loss, Deke had to admit that he did not, at the moment, know his own Bulldogs very well.

14

By game time on Tuesday night, Deke was thanking his good fortune that the Bulldogs' opponents were the Adamsville East Wolverines with their sad record of two victories and six losses.

Standing at the sideline in the Adamsville East gym, Deke watched the players taking their pregame warm-up shots.

Behind Deke, and in front of him across the court, the fans were filling up the rows of bleacher seats. The Adamsville East fans were suffering through a dismal season. But they were turning out for the game and filling the gym. Win or lose, a basketball game in this area of western Illinois was a happening not to be missed. Always, too, there was the hope of a miracle. Perhaps this was the night for the Wolverines to run hot, playing their best game of the season, and the Bulldogs to run cold, spelling upset. Deke knew their feelings. He was fearful they might be right.

The several dozen Bloomfield High rooters who had followed the team's van in an auto caravan were seated together. They were a happy bunch, laughing, chattering, and cheering. They were certain of victory for their Bulldogs. The Wolverines were a weak team. Their record showed it. And the Bulldogs were back at full strength, ready to resume their winning ways.

On the court, Bobby lofted a high, arching shot toward the basket. The ball dropped through the net with a swishing sound.

"Go-Bobby-Go! Go-Bobby-Go!" chanted the Bloomfield fans. The Bloomfield cheerleaders were pumping their hands in rhythm to the chant. For the Bloomfield fans, everything was right with the world.

But Deke knew better. The simple matter of Bobby Haggard's returning to the team from his suspension had not been simple at all.

Deke had been seated on a bench in the locker room, tying his playing shoes, when Bobby showed up for practice. He had felt a sense of relief on two counts. The mere fact of Bobby's appearance answered the primary question in Deke's mind. Was Bobby coming back? Or was Bobby going to change his mind, decide to chuck it all, and forget about basketball? Deke was not sure of the answer until Bobby walked into the locker room.

Beyond that, Deke thought he detected a change in Bobby. There was no sneering half grin on his face. There were no cocky remarks. He was a blank-faced, serious, and subdued Bobby Haggard. Maybe, Deke thought, Bobby had done what he said he had been doing, a lot of thinking. Maybe he had done enough thinking to figure out how to improve his relationship with his teammates. Maybe, Deke thought, we've not only got Bobby Haggard back, but a different and better Bobby Haggard.

Deke nodded a greeting to Bobby, but he did not smile or speak. He was determined to treat Bobby's return as a routine, expectable event, with as little fanfare as possible. From the start, Deke had taken the public position that he assumed Bobby was coming back. There was nothing to gain, and plenty to lose, by indicating anything else now.

As for the subtle signs that Bobby had changed, Deke only hoped he was correct—and hoped the players were receiving the same impression. But Deke was allowed to enjoy his hopes for only a second.

To his credit, Bobby kept his face straight and his mouth shut. Yet in the time it took Bobby to walk to his locker Deke realized there was no change in the attitude of the other players. The locker-room chatter had ended abruptly when Bobby entered. The expressions on the players' faces told the story. Their dislike showed. They were expecting the arrogant half grin and the needling remark. They were bracing for it. Worse yet, there seemed to Deke to be a new ingredient evident in their expressions—embarrassment. After all, they had tried to win without the boy they didn't like, and they had failed. Failure alone was bad enough. It became unbearable when it provided the proof that the Bulldogs needed Bobby Haggard to win the tough games.

With a sudden feeling of alarm, almost panic, Deke realized that his team was a ticking bomb. The players were hiding their embarrassment behind anger. In one sinking moment, Deke knew that if Bobby piped up with the wrong remark, fists might fly.

Clearly, if Bobby Haggard was a changed person after missing the Warfield Tech game, the others were changed for the worse, and they weren't paying any attention to the change in Bobby Haggard.

Deke broke the strained silence quickly. "Let's go," he said. "We've got a lot of work to do today." He finished tying his shoe. Bobby was stripping out of his classroom clothes to get into his practice uniform. So was Chris Santini, another late arrival. The others were almost ready to take the court. "Benjy, you and Skipper head on out and start loosening up. The rest of you, c'mon out when you're ready. And Bobby and Chris, hustle it up, we're running late."

Deke probably did not fool anyone with the tactic, but he decided to change the drawstring at the waist of his sweat pants, keeping him in the locker room until all but Chris and Bobby had left.

The practice session was icy and stiff. Only Chris, irrepressible as always, offered any chatter. The others moved through the drill like robots. They ignored Bobby, playing the game with him when the patterns dictated, but seeming all the while to be looking through him instead of at him.

Bobby took the treatment in stride. He seemed not to notice. He's had plenty of practice, Deke thought.

"You've got a problem, young man," Arnie Hamilton said to Deke at the sideline. The football coach admitted that he could not resist coming in to see if Bobby had returned to the team. "Bobby looks like a changed kid," Arnie said. "But the others aren't giving an inch."

Deke nodded. "They were humiliated by losing to Warfield Tech, with the reason being that Bobby was missing," Deke said. "I was hoping that the weekend would give them time to fix their makeup."

Arnie stood silently for a moment watching the players weave in and out setting up their plays. Then he asked, "What are you going to do about it?"

The question had been ricocheting around in Deke's brain since the team stepped onto the court at the start of practice. Deke had a lot of options open to him, but none seemed to fit the situation. He could call all the players together in the locker room after practice and try to clear the air. But what to say, really? Bobby is changed, let bygones be bygones, think of the team before your own personal feelings? It would not work, and Deke knew it. Articulating the problem was not going to solve it. More likely, talking about it would make matters worse.

Deke could talk with Bobby, extend his support, encourage him to stick it out. But that made no sense. Deke already had warned Bobby that returning to the team was going to be tough for him. No, Bobby was not one to be receptive to anything resembling sympathy.

Deke could talk to the other players and try to win them over. Yet there was no time to deal with the players individually—the basketball season was in full tilt with two games a week, every Tuesday and Friday night—and the idea of a team meeting excluding Bobby was out of the question. That was the worst choice of all. It would put an official stamp of recognition on the fact that Bobby was an outsider. The players would have a harder time accepting him. It would do more to close doors to Bobby than open them.

"Any suggestions?" Deke asked.

Arnie frowned at the players moving around on the court. He was patting his stomach absently with his right hand in his familiar manner. "You've heard that old piece of advice: do something, even if it's wrong."

"Ye-e-s," Deke said slowly. He did not agree with the direction the veteran football coach seemed to be taking. Deke felt that he must know that he was right when he moved against the problem. He must not be wrong. A wrong move could cause irrepairable damage—to the team as a whole, to Bobby, and to the other players as individuals.

"Well, I never believed that piece of advice myself," Arnie said. "Especially when dealing with youngsters. I think that sometimes the best thing to do at the moment is—nothing, nothing at all. Let things settle into place before you wade in. Then you'll know where you're going. Oh, sure, the world is full of people who will accuse you of being indecisive. Pay no attention to them. The team is not their responsibility. The players, for all their problems, are out there playing together right now. Things could be worse. Probably will be. They may reach a crisis point—an explosion—and then surprise you by settling the problem themselves. By themselves, that is, with your invisible help."

"That's what I thought," Deke said. "But I wasn't sure."

Arnie cocked his head, looked up at the taller Deke, and smiled. "Oh, I'm not sure either," he said. "I never am."

Deke moved back onto the court to join the players in the practice session, still unsettled, still unsure, but less so than before. He would wait and see.

Later in the drill, in the closing minutes, Herbie Foxx appeared in the gym.

"Great, great!" he exulted, when Deke joined him at the sideline. "We'll slaughter Adamsville East tomorrow night—and then on to the Mount Perry game."

With some surprise, Deke realized that Herbie's elation at seeing Bobby Haggard back in uniform was blinding him to the signs of trouble so obvious to both Deke and Arnie. "I hope you're right," Deke said.

Herbie cast a questioning look at Deke.

Herbie's words echoed in Deke's mind as he stepped forward to greet his players for the final word before the opening tip-off. It won't be a slaughter, Deke thought. The Bulldogs will win, to be sure. The luck of the draw in scheduling was presenting them with one of the weaker teams of the area tonight. The Bulldogs, despite their troubles, were the vastly superior team. They were sure to prevail. But Deke knew that they were going to have to pay the price for things not being right with the team. There was a stiffness, an edginess—yes, an unhappiness—that bodes ill for a basketball team.

"Concentrate, concentrate," Deke said, as he and the players clasped hands and pumped once in the center of the huddle. "Make every play count."

15

Benjy Holman outjumped the Adamsville East center and easily flicked the ball to his left, into the waiting hands of Skipper Denham.

On the bench, Deke was surprised. Benjy, in complete control of the game's opening tip-off, could have passed the ball to anyone. The choice was his. Bobby Haggard was standing to Benjy's right. Bobby should have been Benjy's choice. That was where the tip should have gone. But Benjy sent it to his left, to Skipper.

Skipper took in Benjy's tip, pivoted and dribbled twice, and passed the ball off to Ken Flaherty back near the center stripe. Benjy was moving into position in front of the basket. Ken passed to Dennis North at the sideline. Dennis dribbled down the sideline, toward the corner. He turned and stopped, looking at the field before him. The Adamsville East guard waved his hands in front of Dennis. Quickly Dennis faked a set shot. The Adamsville East guard reacted by throwing his hands up. Dennis sent a low bounce pass under the guard's arms to Benjy on the outside post. Benjy took in the pass, dribbled once, and turned. Going up as he turned, Benjy hooked the ball into the basket—swish!—over the outstretched hands of a helpless guard.

Deke glanced at the scoreboard instinctively: Wolverines 0, Visitors 2. Four of his players—all but one, Bobby Haggard—had handled the ball on the way to the game's first field goal. Deke turned his attention back to the action on the court.

The Wolverines brought the ball down the court cautiously. They were a deliberate, careful basketball team. They set up their plays with a precision that Deke admired. Short of talent, the Wolverines were doomed to a losing season. But it was readily evident that they were a well-coached team. The players knew their jobs.

The little guard dribbling the ball across the center stripe was the signal caller for the Wolverines. He was waving with his free hand as he dribbled, sending a teammate a few paces over to the left. It was smart basketball. The shift pulled Dennis out a few feet, stretching the Bulldogs' zone.

With everyone in place and ready finally, the Wolverines began their weaving motion designed to screen for the outside shooters and set up lanes for the dribblers to race in for lay-up shots. As the play shaped up, Deke could see what was coming. The Wolverines were luring the Bulldogs' zone defense a step forward, to open the way for a pass under the basket. The first stage had caused Dennis to move out. Now others were taking the bait. Deke leaned forward. He wondered if any of his Bulldogs realized what was taking place.

Suddenly the little guard shouted a number. He was dribbling toward the sideline. He stopped, turned, and rifled a pass to the center under the basket. Benjy caught himself a half step out of position. He tried to correct himself, but it was too late. The center went up and laid it in.

Deke unconsciously nodded his approval at the perfection of the play.

He sought out Benjy among the players rushing back down the court. Benjy nodded slightly. Deke knew that Benjy was not going to allow himself to be trapped that way again. Benjy knew what had happened. He would be ready next time.

Ken took the ball from the referee out-of-bounds under the basket and flipped a pass inbounds to Bobby to resume the play. The Wolverines dropped back into their defensive positions. Bobby dribbled easily across the center stripe.

In the bleachers behind Deke the Bloomfield High fans began the chant: "Go-Bobby-Go! Go-Bobby-Go!"

Bobby passed to Skipper at his left and moved over in front of him, heading for the sideline. Bobby was looking back, obviously expecting a return pass.

But Skipper turned and handed off to Dennis moving

the other way. Dennis almost lost the ball to a tenacious guard, then succeeded in passing back to Skipper, who sent a high pass toward Benjy in front of the basket.

The pass was slightly off target, and the ball brushed past Benjy's outstretched hands. It bounced out-of-bounds.

Deke got to his feet. The players were freezing Bobby out. That was obvious. They were keeping the ball away from him. First, on the game's opening tip-off, Benjy had chosen to send the ball to Skipper. Then in the passes that followed, everybody but Bobby got a hand on the ball. In this last play, Bobby brought the ball up the court, but never touched it again.

The Wolverines were bringing the ball back down the court. The Bulldogs were falling back into their defensive positions.

Briefly Deke's eyes met Bobby's as he backpedaled to set himself for the Wolverines' attack. Bobby's quick glance told Deke: Bobby knows. It was not a questioning glance. Not even a puzzled or hurt glance. Bobby was angry.

The other Bulldogs, moving back down the court, did not look at Deke as they went past.

Deke sat down again. He had no choice but to wait. He could not call a time-out when the opposing team had possession of the ball. The freeze-out was the ultimate retaliation for the weeks of jibes, sneers, and contemptuous stares Bobby Haggard had given his teammates.

The thoughts tumbled through Deke's mind. Almost always a freeze-out is a conspiracy. Some of the players —two or three or four of them—get together and decide to exclude a player. Deke found it hard to visualize Benjy or Skipper or any of the others plotting damage to their own team. Sure, the loss to Warfield Tech hurt and disappointed them all. They blamed Bobby for letting the team down. The loss was embarrassing, too. But Deke could not bring himself to believe that their anger, their hurt, their embarrassment had led them to join a plan to wreck the team.

Occasionally a freeze-out develops its own momentum. Nobody conspires. Nobody says a word. But the individual players decide on their own, perhaps unconsciously, to ignore a player they dislike. The freeze-out develops out of a natural human preference to play the game with friends. They pass the ball to a player they like. They set up a friend for a score, not the player they dislike.

Either way, the situation is bad business. A coach cannot tolerate it. But what to do? Deke, seated forward, elbows on his knees, hands clasped, frowned at the question.

He could call a time-out at the earliest opportunity and lash them with words. That might jolt them enough to end the freeze. He could bench a leading player—Benjy or Skipper—and warn the others that the same fate awaited them if the freeze did not stop. He could wait and see if the heat of the game itself could thaw the freeze-out.

One thing Deke could not do was pull Bobby out of the game. That was out of the question. Benching Bobby would amount to bowing to the blatant challenge of the other players. True, in many ways Bobby was more to blame for the freeze than any of the players ignoring him. But Bobby must remain in the game. Otherwise, Deke was surrendering his authority as the coach.

The action on the court brought Deke back from his thoughts.

Bobby, caught in a screening maneuver by the Wolverines, was stabbing out a hand in a wild reach for the ball as a dribbler went by. He got a piece of the ball. It was enough to break the dribbler's rhythm. The dribbler was forced to halt and try to regain control of the ball. Bobby, carried forward by the momentum of his thrust for the ball, was coming around the man who was screening him out. Bobby's quickness afoot brought him alongside the dribbler, now juggling the ball in a frantic effort to hold on.

In a flash, Bobby moved past, deftly took the ball out of the befuddled player's hands, and broke into a dribble toward the center stripe. Skipper, moving from the sideline, broke into a sprint for the basket, his left hand in the air, waggling a signal for a pass. Bobby looked up as he crossed the center stripe. He saw Skipper. Still on the run, Bobby brought the ball up in both hands and sent a high pass half the length of the court.

Skipper and the ball reached the corridor in front of the basket at the same instant. He pulled in the ball, dribbled once, and went up. The ball came off the backboard and rolled around the rim of the basket.

Then it dropped through.

Skipper's forward motion carried him under the basket and off the court. He crashed into the pads on the end wall, cushioning his collision with outstretched hands.

Skipper was not within sight of the basket when the ball finally quit its gently rolling tour of the rim and fell through the hoop. He turned from the crash pads on the end wall with a questioning look on his face. Had he scored?

Bobby, continuing his forward rush toward the basket to rebound in case the shot rolled off the rim, was grinning. He shot a triumphant fist into the air. Skipper grinned back at him.

Deke, on his feet when the play exploded, watched the scene. For an instant, Skipper and Bobby were teammates who, thanks to each other, had marked up two points for the Bulldogs. In that instant, forgotten were the cutting remarks and the cocky half grin that Skipper resented. Also forgotten were Bobby's convictions that Skipper was a snob who looked down on him.

Deke decided not to call a time-out before the resumption of play. He sat down to watch. Perhaps the single play had been enough to thaw a freeze-out. Deke had seen miracles wrought on the basketball court by the electric excitement of one scoring play. Perhaps. . . .

But as the minutes of the first quarter ticked away, Deke saw the evidence time and again. The Bulldogs were passing to Bobby when they had to. Trapped, with only Bobby in sight and free, they gave him the ball. Otherwise, they turned and handed off the ball or passed to another teammate.

Finally, the first quarter ended.

The scoreboard read: Wolverines 14, Visitors 17.

16

By the time the players were coming off the court for the first-quarter intermission, Deke had decided on his course.

Deke looked each of his five starters in the eye when they gathered around him at the bench. First, Skipper. The senior forward returned the gaze blankly. Neither defiance nor guilt showed in his eyes. Then Benjy, the other senior on the starting five. The tall player was breathing heavily. His eyes met Deke's for an instant. Then Benjy reached down and picked up a towel. Bobby's mouth was a straight line and his eyes, squinted into narrow slits, showed his anger. For once he's keeping his mouth shut, Deke thought. Ken Flaherty and Dennis North shuffled nervously. Ken flickered a trace of a tight, quick, little smile when Deke looked at him. Dennis kept his gaze on the floor, busying himself with hitching up his trunks.

"You know what you're doing, I assume," Deke snapped. He spoke in low tones. This was no time for shouting. But in his anger he bit off each of the words sharply. "You're losing a game and quite possibly destroying your entire season. That's what you're doing."

A three-piece combo at the end of the gym was blaring a fight song. The cheerleaders for both schools were on the court, exhorting their fans. Deke was grateful for the noise drowning out the sound of his words beyond the circle of players.

"Now, let me tell you what I am going to do," Deke said. He fixed his eyes on Skipper. He lifted a finger and pointed at Skipper. "You're first, Skipper."

Skipper's eyebrow shot up.

"The first time that I think any of you—any of you—is still freezing Bobby out, you—you, Skipper—are coming out of the game—out, for keeps. You will spend the rest of the game on the bench."

Skipper frowned but said nothing. The other players glanced at each other.

"Do you understand, all of you?" Deke asked, glancing around the group. They all nodded, all but Bobby. He did not move. Bobby's face remained locked in tight-lipped, squint-eyed anger.

Deke turned to Ken. "And you are second, Ken." Deke pointed a finger at the little guard. "If Skipper gets pulled out of the game because somebody—any of you —is freezing Bobby out, you're the next one—through, out for the night."

Ken blinked and looked at Skipper. He seemed to be asking for guidance.

"We will go all the way down the line," Deke said. "All the way down the line."

Deke straightened to his full six feet, seven inches. He hitched his trousers. The cheerleaders were moving off the court. Deke glanced up at the clock. Time for the short intermission was running out.

He ran a hand nervously over his short brush-cut hair and leaned into the circle of players. "Forget about the old troubles, and play the way you know you can," he said. The sharp edge to his voice was gone. He let his eyes meet Bobby's for a moment. Deke's words were meant for all of them. But Bobby most of all needed to be listening. Bobby's anger, and perhaps hurt, were understandable. But it was imperative that he not add to the justification for the freeze by even so much as a grin. "Play the way you know you can," Deke repeated. "You'll be the happier for it tomorrow morning . . . and the happier for it for the rest of your lives."

Automatically, woodenly, Deke and the players performed the ritual handclasp in the center of the circle and pumped once. The players moved onto the court, and Deke stepped back and sat down on the bench.

He glanced at the scoreboard: a three-point lead. Adamsville East, as weak as it was, could close the gap and win the game if the worst happened to the Bulldogs.

And the worst that could happen, Deke figured, was

not the players freezing out Bobby. The freeze was ended. Deke was sure of it. He had guaranteed them a defeat if the freeze continued. He had promised that Skipper would be pulled from the game at the first sign that any of them was freezing out Bobby. And then Ken. And then all the others, one by one. No, the freeze was ended. The players might have thought they could win this game without Bobby, but they had too much pride, Deke was sure, to send themselves intentionally down to defeat. The worst that could happen was a listless, spiritless, mechanical performance. Deke knew the signs: players moving about stiffly, fumbling, committing mental errors, spoiling plays. And there were passes that spelled trouble, heavy passes. The ball comes in with no spin, dropping, a deadweight ball. The lack of zip in the passes is contagious. Next, the shooters lose their fine edge of accuracy. A half-inch off means a miss. Disaster is built of such things.

The Bulldogs got an unexpected break at the start of the second quarter, thanks to the Adamsville East coach outsmarting himself. The Wolverines shifted into a new defense, virtually ignoring Bobby on the outside.

Deke knew what was going on in the opposing coach's mind. No brilliance was required to spot that in the first quarter Bobby was not getting the ball. Bobby was the hottest shooter on the Bulldogs' team, and clearly the main target of the defense in normal circumstances. But Bobby was being frozen out. The Wolverines were wasting their defense trying to contain a player who never had a chance to shoot. An adjustment had been in order, to be sure.

But Deke was surprised by the extent of the Wolverines' defensive shift. They pulled themselves close in under the basket, concentrating their defense on Benjy. It was a lopsided alignment with strength off to one side, the side where Skipper normally took his shots from the corner.

The Wolverines' change in their defense had taken for granted that the freeze was not going to end.

But it did, and Bobby, unhindered at the edge of the keyhole, pumped in four quick field goals before the Wolverines called time-out to reconsider their strategy.

The scoreboard showed the Bulldogs leading 25–16 when the players approached the bench. But nobody was smiling, including Deke. He had seen enough in the first few minutes of the second quarter to know that his Bulldogs were headed for trouble. They were going to need every one of those nine points of lead before the game ended. They were going through the motions of playing, without sparkle, without fire.

By the half-time intermission, the Bulldogs' lead was cut to six points, 34–28. The Wolverines' realization that the freeze had ended put the defensive pressure back on Bobby. His scoring rampage was slowed.

Deke did not mention the freeze in the dressing room at the half time. What was there to say? He did not point out the lackluster play of the second quarter. The players certainly knew about it as well as he.

Instead, Deke moved into a technical analysis. He suggested ways the Bulldogs might convert the Wolverines' shortcomings into points. He dealt with the individual play of the Bulldogs in coping with their counterparts on the Adamsville East team. Everybody listened with blank expressions.

The third quarter, and then the fourth, finally dragged to a finish, and the Bulldogs escaped with a victory, 56–50.

"You were lucky to win," Deke told the players in the dressing room, "and you know it."

They looked more like losers than winners as they peeled off their game uniforms and headed for the showers. The look of anger, with hurt mixed in, remained on Bobby's face. Still, he was keeping his silence, and Deke could ask for no more from him at this point. Deke thought he detected signs of embarrassment in the faces of some, Skipper and Dennis in particular. He did not know whether they were embarrassed about the freeze-out or the overall poor performance.

Undoubtedly, they had a lot of thinking to do, and they needed to do it quickly, with Mount Perry right around the corner.

For now, Deke's mind could not shake the dread of the drive back to Bloomfield. This was going to be a good night to be done with.

17

The thirty-five-mile ride in the darkened van carrying the Bulldogs back to Bloomfield was a silent, grim ordeal.

At the wheel of the van, Deke was grateful for the driving chore. It relieved him of the need to sit in back with the players. He did not want to be a part of the somber crowd. He concentrated on staring out of the windshield into the black night. The van's headlights were glistening on the wet blacktop road and shining on the piles of snow alongside it. He busied himself keeping a sharp eye out for icy patches.

On the seats behind Deke, the players were a glum lot. There was none of the laughter, joking, and chatter that a winning team is expected to enjoy. The Bulldogs might have been the losers, for all the fun they were having.

Chris Santini, always ready with a wisecrack and a laugh, tried once as the van was rolling out of the Adamsville East parking lot to begin the drive home. "Well, it beats losing," he said.

Silence.

Then there was a slight shuffling movement. Somebody was turning in his seat to glare Chris into silence. Nobody wanted to talk.

"Okay, okay," Chris finally said, and he sank into a silence of his own.

Deke, in the driver's seat, did nothing to try to change the mood of the players. Perhaps the players needed the silence. Perhaps they needed to be stuck with their own reflections.

In the rearview mirror, Deke could see the headlights of the auto caravan of the Bloomfield High fans following the team home. Their team had won. They were a happy crowd. They just didn't know, Deke thought.

The rhythmic chant of the fans—"Go-Bobby-Go! Go-Bobby-Go!"—was still ringing in Deke's ears. But never once during the game did Bobby respond to the cheers with a smile or an uplifted fist as in earlier games. The angry look never left his face. He was wearing it when he changed clothes in the dressing room after the game. He was wearing it when he climbed aboard the van and took a seat alone at the rear.

The look of anger was better than the old half grin, Deke figured. And Bobby, to his credit, had kept his mouth shut through it all—the playing time, the half-time intermission, the time in the dressing room after the game, and now in the van. Bobby had obviously made up his mind to change his ways. He was sticking to it, even if the other players failed to notice or acknowledge the change.

Deke remembered Arnie Hamilton's words: "They may reach a crisis point—an explosion—and then settle the problem themselves."

Maybe so, Deke thought. Maybe it's true that nothing clears the air like an explosion.

The van, arriving in Bloomfield, rolled through the darkened streets and slowed at an intersection. A block farther, it turned into the Bloomfield High parking lot.

A half-dozen cars were parked in the well-lit lot. The friends and parents who had not driven to the game were waiting to pick up players. Behind the van, a couple of cars remaining from the caravan pulled into the lot.

By the time Deke pulled the van to a halt, people were streaming out of their cars, crowding around the van in the wintry night. Their breath made little clouds of vapor visible in the glare of the parking-lot lights.

Deke was the first to step out of the van. He was met with a roaring cheer from the small crowd. He managed a grin and waved. The cheer from the elated fans felt good, no matter what problems were brewing.

Behind Deke, each of the players stepping out of the van in single file got a loud cheer from the crowd. Deke watched them, one by one.

Skipper gave a tight-lipped smile and a small wave. Benjy ignored the cheer completely, scanning the crowd for his parents. The other players gestured slightly, unsmiling, in automatic reaction to the cheer. Oddly, Chris wore the most troubled expression of all. He was used to laughing.

The problems of the Bulldogs were there, clearly evident, on the face of every boy stepping off the van. Perhaps later, at home, the parents would notice that something was wrong. They might ask about it. They might be told. But for now the excited Bloomfield fans standing in the cold night greeting their team were not looking for any problems, and they saw none.

The last player out of the van's door was Bobby Haggard, from his seat alone at the rear.

The cheers of the fans hit a high pitch. Somebody shouted, "Go-Bobby-Go!" The crowd took up the chant.

Bobby gave a small wave and, unsmiling, walked around in front of the van.

In the glare of the headlights, Deke recognized the boys meeting Bobby—Phil Metzger and Bill Hainey. Bobby broke into a jogging stride toward them. Deke stared at Bobby's back moving away from him.

Phil Metzger called out something to Bobby, and Bobby waved. Then the three of them piled into a car. There were others waiting in the car. With a screech of the tires, the car raced out of the parking lot.

Deke parked and locked the team's van and drove home in his car, but his night was far from finished. Long afterward, he sat at his kitchenette table, sipping a glass of milk in his pajamas, staring out the window.

He wished that Bobby's changed attitude had come earlier. He wished that when it did come, it had not been met with a freeze-out. But most of all, he wished that Bobby's changed attitude had also included a change of friends.

The next morning Deke arrived at the school early, as always. The corridors were empty when he walked through, pulling off his gloves and stuffing them in his overcoat pocket as he went. The first students would not be arriving for a half hour.

Deke yawned. It had been a short, restless night. He had a busy day ahead of him. This was Wednesday. Only today and tomorrow remained for the plotting and the practicing for the important game against the Mount Perry Tigers. His notebook full of jottings on the Tigers awaited him in his office. Out of the scribbled observations and ideas must come the strategy for victory.

But to make the strategy work—to convert Deke's pencil markings into triumph in the game—the Bulldogs needed an extraordinary amount of that great intangible called teamwork. The thought brought a frown to Deke's face as he turned and headed down the stairs toward his office.

The Bulldogs' display of teamwork against Adamsville East was hardly encouraging. A freeze-out of one player was the ultimate in dissension—the exact opposite of effective teamwork. Even after the freeze-out ended, the Bulldogs played a stiff, mechanical game. The missing ingredient, still, was teamwork. Their play was not the stuff of victory over a tough opponent. No, the Bulldog team that played Adamsville East, despite the victory, was doomed to defeat—possibly humiliating defeat—against Mount Perry.

Unless, that is, the Bulldogs found a way to get themselves together, and quickly.

Deke unlocked his office door, stepped inside, and dropped his overcoat on a chair. He walked around his desk and stood for a moment, leafing through the pages of notes on the Mount Perry Tigers.

"Any basketball team can be defeated," he told himself, as he looked down at the penciled scribblings. If the Bulldogs could pull themselves together and function as a team, the secret to beating Mount Perry was buried somewhere in all of that scrawling.

"Coach?"

The tentative question came from the doorway, softly spoken.

Deke, startled, looked up.

Skipper was standing in the door, his books under his arm, his heavy jacket still buttoned to the neck. Behind Skipper, and looming larger, was Benjy.

"Yes, what is it?"

"May we see you for a minute before the classes start?"

Deke waved the two players inside his small office. He stepped around the desk and retrieved his overcoat from the chair. Skipper and Benjy took seats. Deke tossed his overcoat onto a rack and sat down at his desk.

Deke studied the two players for a moment. They were a somber pair. This must be serious. And here they were at school more than thirty minutes ahead of the bell for the first class. That meant they had planned the meeting with the coach, knowing he always arrived early. This was no casual drop-in visit and no coincidence that the two of them had arrived together.

Deke frowned briefly at the thought that they might be in his office to announce they were quitting the team. He had moved hard and fast against the freeze-out of Bobby. They had resented Bobby's behavior from the start. Now they might be resenting Deke's action in protecting Bobby against the freeze-out.

"What's up?" Deke asked.

Skipper unbuttoned his jacket and leaned forward.

"Coach, we—well, I mean some of us—did a little talking last night, over at Benjy's house, after we got back to Bloomfield from the game."

Deke waited without speaking. He hoped for the best yet feared the worst. He tried to put an expression of pleasant interest, but not serious concern, on his face. He knew he was not succeeding entirely.

"Benjy and I are seniors," Skipper said. "The only seniors. Well, that is, the only seniors on the starting five. And, well, that's why we're the ones who are here."

Deke almost smiled. He never had seen Skipper Denham fumble for words. Skipper usually was the articulate, affirmative, effective speaker, no matter the situation. He addressed school assemblies, sometimes off the cuff, as easily as he chatted with a friend walking along the corridors. But not this morning. Skipper was having trouble getting the words out.

"What is it you want to say?" Deke asked. He tried to

ask the question easily, to reassure the senior forward who was the team's leader. But Deke knew that his own anxiety showed in the tone of his voice.

Skipper straightened himself in the chair. "Well, first, let me tell you that there was no organized effort to freeze Bobby Haggard out last night. We didn't plan it. It just happened. We all knew what was happening, and we went along with it. But there was no plan in advance to do it."

"I'm glad to hear that's the way it was," Deke said.

"It started with Benjy on the opening tip-off," Skipper said. He paused and glanced at Benjy, obviously offering Benjy the opportunity to tell his part of the story himself. Benjy said nothing. "Benjy just thought, Why tip it over to that guy and give him a break? So he sent the tip to me. I was surprised. But I understood why Benjy had done it. Then, well, it seemed that everybody just understood."

Deke nodded and waited. There had to be more to come.

"Well, it won't happen again," Skipper said.

Benjy nodded.

"Good," Deke said, and again he waited. Neither player was making any move to leave. They had come to say more than this.

"He seems to have changed," Skipper said suddenly.

"I noticed it, too." Deke said. "But I thought after last night that the change had escaped your attention."

"We talked about it," Skipper said slowly, feeling his way for the right words. "We talked about it. I guess that the change first showed on Monday. He seemed to want to be a part of the team, one of us. But to tell you the truth, nobody believed it. But we saw it again last night. He never popped off or put that look on his face—you know what I mean—even when everybody was freezing him out."

"Yes, I know."

"Well, if he stays changed—you know, no more of all that guff he hands out—well, then we'll make it with him without any trouble."

Deke looked at Skipper, then at Benjy. "All of you?" he asked finally.

"All of us," Skipper said.

Deke looked at Benjy again. He knew that Benjy carried a vivid memory of Bobby's racial slur shouted at a black teammate last season.

Benjy seemed to understand the question in Deke's eyes. He nodded soberly. "He seems different," Benjy said.

"Good," Deke said. He leaned back in his chair and looked at his wristwatch. "You'd better head upstairs. The bell for the first classes is going to ring in a few minutes."

Skipper and Benjy got to their feet. They stood in place for a moment and exchanged glances briefly.

Then Skipper spoke. "And, Coach. . . ."

"Yes?"

"There's one other thing I have to say."

Deke waited.

"We've all talked about it, and we all know that maybe

we haven't been fair. Bobby didn't help the situation, the way he always acted. But it wasn't all his fault. And we all know it."

"There are always two sides," Deke said. "Let's hope that we've got it behind us now and can concentrate on the game of basketball. We've got a big one coming up Friday night. It's going to take everything we've got."

The two players left.

Deke stared through the empty doorway for a moment. Then he leaned forward in the chair and exhaled a long breath of air. He stretched his long arms out to the sides, then brought them forward and laid his palms, fingers spread, flat on the notes about Mount Perry.

His face broke into a wide grin.

18

The elation was short-lived. It ended a few minutes after ten thirty with the ringing of the telephone on Deke's desk.

Deke frowned at the interruption. He was sailing through the notes on the Mount Perry team. The meeting with Skipper and Benjy had put an entirely new value on the notes. The carefully devised battle plan was not going to be for nothing. The players were going to be ready for the game. The Bulldogs were going to be a team. All that was left was to draw the strategy and drill the team in the intricacies of the plan. Two practice sessions remained—today and tomorrow—and they were all that Deke and his Bulldogs were going to need.

"Yes," Deke said into the telephone.

He half expected to hear the staccato voice of Herbie Foxx. The sportscaster could not have failed to spot the freeze-out of Bobby in the game the night before. Herbie was going to be calling about it.

"Coach, Wilfred Mulholland here," came the voice on the telephone.

Deke felt a slight shudder of alarm as he heard the principal's voice. He remembered the last time his telephone had rung with the principal on the other end of the line.

"Good morning, sir," Deke said.

"Coach Warden, I'm afraid you are not going to think so."

Deke frowned as his feeling of alarm grew. "Oh?" he piped.

"It's more of the Bobby Haggard problem," Mulholland said.

"I'll be right in," Deke said.

Deke knotted his necktie, pulled on his jacket, and headed for the principal's office, taking the steps three at a time. With some effort he held himself to a normal walk through the corridor and past the classrooms.

Mulholland wasted no time getting to the point when Deke was seated across the desk in the principal's office. "Do you happen to know where Bobby Haggard is?" Mulholland asked.

"No, I—" Deke said, then interrupted himself. "Isn't he here, in class?"

"No, he isn't, and that is the problem."

"I don't understand."

Deke's mind flashed back to the night before—the grimly set mouth, the angry eyes, the silence so unlike the Bobby Haggard he had known.

"He is absent from school," Mulholland said. He reached out and picked up a pencil and tapped the desk top lightly. "Normally, we don't run a check on a student marked absent from his first class. With most of our students, it simply means that they are ill and staying home. We know that a parent will be phoning during the morning to explain. We don't start calling the home until noon, if we haven't heard. But with Bobby Haggard's record—well, he's been a truant once this fall already, you know, and he was a recurring problem all last year. I thought it prudent in his case to check immediately. We got no answer at his home. We had the devil of a time tracking down his mother where she works. She knew nothing. She said he left home this morning for school as usual."

Deke listened to Mulholland's dry recital of the facts with a horrible feeling of helplessness. Finally he said, more as a question than a statement, "Maybe there's been an accident."

Mulholland sighed and kept tapping the pencil lightly on the desk. "I doubt it," he said. Then, after a pause, he added, "And you doubt it, too."

"Yes," Deke said absently. In the event of an accident, Bobby's mother or the school, or both, would have been notified by this time.

Mulholland was looking Deke in the eye. "If everything is the way it appears to be," he said, "I will have no choice at this point but to sentence him to the early morning study hall and withdraw his participation in extracurricular activities."

Deke nodded slowly. He knew the rules. There was a limit to what the school administration could put up with and still allow a student to play a hero's role in extracurricular activities. Deke was not surprised by Mulholland's decision. Basketball was an adjunct to education at Bloomfield High, not vice versa.

"I have no choice," Mulholland repeated.

"I understand," Deke said.

Deke walked slowly along the corridor back to his office. He cursed the timing of the events. Things had come close to falling into place. But now it was clear that close was not enough. Bobby had changed his attitude. But the change had come too late. By the time Bobby had changed, the other players were in a mood to freeze him out of a game, and they did it, before they recognized that he had changed. Now Skipper and Benjy and the others were ready to give him a new chance. But this, too, came too late. Before Bobby had had a chance to learn of it, he was in new trouble.

At the foot of the stairs leading down to his office, Deke heard his telephone ringing.

"Have you heard about Bobby Haggard?" It was the voice of Herbie Foxx.

"I—" Deke said, and then he stopped himself. The sportscaster could not possibly know of Bobby's truancy before Wilfred Mulholland had. He could not possibly know what Mulholland was planning to do. Mulholland had only just told Deke. He would not tell Herbie before he told Deke, even if Herbie called him. "What are you talking about?" Deke asked.

"I thought you probably hadn't heard, and it's important," Herbie said. "You ought to know about this."

"Ought to know about what?"

"Bobby and some of his friends got themselves arrested last night. They spent a while in jail."

"Jail!"

"I got the story from our news director. He picked it up this morning making his regular rounds."

"What happened?"

"Seems they got themselves stopped for speeding. Then it turned out some of the crowd had been drinking. With further investigation, a couple of marijuana cigarettes were found in the car. The officer hauled in the whole crowd."

"I wish I had known. . . ."

"Funny, that," Herbie said. "Bobby didn't want you to know. He begged the desk sergeant not to let the word get out, so you wouldn't hear about it. The desk sergeant finally agreed. It was no problem. After all, Bobby himself was not formally charged with anything. He was booked, but just on disorderly conduct because he happened to be in the crowd. He hadn't been drinking, and the pot was not on his person."

Deke considered for a moment telling Herbie about the truancy problem. But he decided against it. Instead, he asked, "Do you have to go on the air with this?"

"We don't normally name juvenile offenders," Herbie said.

Deke sighed.

"You noticed the freeze-out of Bobby in the first quarter last night," Deke said. He was sure Herbie had recognized the freeze for what it was. He had a good reason for bringing up the subject.

"How could I miss it?"

"I think that we've got all of that kind of trouble straightened out," Deke said, "and I need your cooperation."

"What?" Herbie sounded suspicious.

"No mention of the freeze-out on the air," Deke said. "No commentaries on the subject. No reference to it at all. Just don't stir things up right now."

There was a pause at Herbie's end of the line. Then he said, "Okay."

Deke hung up the telephone slowly. He still was standing where he had picked up the ringing telephone when he walked into his office. He was across the desk from his chair, his back to the door. He sensed a movement behind him, and he turned.

Bobby Haggard was standing in the office doorway.

19

"Coach, I. . . ."

There was no smile, cocky or otherwise, on Bobby's face. His mouth was a thin, straight line. Not the tight-lipped expression of anger that he wore through the Adamsville East game, but a sad line of hopelessness. His large, brown eyes were wide, not squinty slits of anger, and they were no longer darting from object to object with the wary alertness of a fox surviving in the forest. He stared, almost blankly, at Deke. Somehow, standing there in the doorway, Bobby looked even smaller than his slender five feet, seven inches.

"Come in, Bobby. Sit down."

Bobby, carrying his books in his right hand, stepped inside Deke's office and perched himself on the edge of the wooden chair alongside the desk. He put his books on the floor at his feet. He unzipped his jacket.

Deke closed the office door.

Walking back around to his chair behind the desk, Deke recalled the last time he closed the door for a meeting with Bobby Haggard. Quite a difference this time. There was no wisecrack now: "Wow! This must be hot, closed door and all." This time there was only silence from Bobby Haggard.

Deke sat down at his desk and waited.

"It's all blown now, isn't it?" Bobby said.

Deke ignored the question. "Tell me what happened," he said.

"What?"

"I know about the arrest," Deke said.

Bobby let out a breath of air. He seemed relieved that the matter was in the open. "I figured you would know," he said. "I tried to talk them into keeping it quiet. But when I got up this morning, I just knew that the word was going to get out. I knew that you would find out about it. And I knew what you would think, and what all the players would think. The way it makes the team look, and all. . . ."

Bobby met Deke's gaze as he spoke, but he shifted his eyes to a spot on the wall behind Deke when he let his voice trail off.

Deke let the silence rest for a moment. Bobby was

right, of course. Skipper and Benjy and Dennis—all of them—were a pretty straitlaced bunch. They did not cut classes. They did not explode firecrackers in the school. And they did not get themselves mixed up with the police. Clearly, too, they did not like those who did those things. The fact had made Bobby an outsider from the start. Now, at the time that Bobby seemed to have changed, and the other players seemed ready to accept Bobby, everything was collapsing like a house of cards.

"Tell me what happened," Deke repeated.

Bobby looked back at Deke. "It was all a mistake. Really. A mistake."

"Let me hear about it."

The words poured out of Bobby in a rush. "I didn't have anything to drink in the car last night—or any time. Some of the others did. But I didn't. They were needling me about not drinking. That's how we came to be speeding in the first place. They just goosed up the speed and said they would keep going faster and faster until I took a drink. But I didn't. I was wishing that I could get out of the car. But I couldn't. It was speeding. And I don't know anything—not anything at all—about any marijuana cigarettes in the car. The police said they found some. But I don't know anything about it. Nothing. Honest. Really. That's the truth. All of it—it's the truth."

Bobby stopped speaking as suddenly as he had started. He was breathing heavily. Partly the torrent of words had left him winded. But also, Deke was sure, the boy was excited. Bobby's eyes reflected a mixture of pleading and hopelessness.

"So you decided to skip school today," Deke said. He spoke the words softly.

Bobby seemed for a moment to be reaching for words. "I just couldn't face it," he said finally. "I knew when I got up this morning that it was not going to work, trying to keep it quiet, and all of that. I knew that everybody was going to know about it. . . ."

"Where have you been all morning?"

"I just walked around until I knew that my mother and father had left for work. Then I went home. I was there when the telephone rang. I knew it was the school. They were looking for me. I just let it ring. I didn't answer it." He paused. "I've just been hanging around the house."

"And now you're here." Deke made a statement of fact, but he was asking a question, requesting an explanation, an elaboration in Bobby's own words.

Bobby shrugged. "Yeah, I'm here," he said. "I finally figured out that I couldn't stay away forever. I was going to have to come back sometime. So I'm here."

Deke watched Bobby closely. Maybe all was not lost. After all, Bobby was here. He was tardy, but no longer a truant. That would become true the moment he appeared in class. And, most encouraging of all to Deke, Bobby was in his coach's office. Bobby was looking, hoping, for another chance at fitting in with the basketball team. What was it Bobby had said at the outset? "It's all blown now." Well, maybe not.

But Deke did not say so to Bobby.

Instead, he leaned forward and told Bobby, "You should not have been in that car in the first place. You should have known that it could lead to trouble. You've been in trouble with that crowd before—cutting classes, throwing firecrackers in the classroom. You don't need their kind of trouble. You don't need those kinds of friends."

"Friends," Bobby said slowly. The word seemed to come hard to him. "They're the only friends I've got. You don't think that those snobs on the team—"

"Wait a minute," Deke snapped. "Stop right there." Deke paused. Bobby waited. "It may very well be true that the boys on the team never gave you the chance you think you deserved. You may be right. But it's also true that you never gave them a chance to like you."

A hint of the cocky half grin appeared, then vanished. Bobby's eyes began darting around, then stopped.

"I made up my mind when I came back after the Warfield Tech game to change," Bobby said. "And you saw what happened. They were freezing me out of the game. Do you call that—"

Deke waved a hand. "Hold it a minute. Did it ever occur to you that perhaps they, all of them, are sorry about the freeze? Did it ever occur to you that by now, this morning, they all regret the freeze even more than you and I?"

"I don't see—"

"I can tell you that they are sorry, and they do regret it, and they do want to find a way to make up for it, if it's possible to make up for it at this stage of things."

Bobby said nothing. He lifted an eyebrow.

"They've told me so," Deke said softly. "And they told me without my having to ask them."

Deke leaned back in his chair and let the impact of his statement sink in on Bobby. He had no intention of mentioning names. Bobby did not need to know that Skipper and Benjy did the talking. He did not need to wonder if they really spoke for the whole team. He needed only to know that there was, indeed, a possibility of another chance for him.

If. . . .

If Wilfred Mulholland would agree to reverse himself on the decision to prohibit Bobby's participation in varsity basketball. If the players stuck by their promise in the wake of Bobby's latest brush with trouble.

"The first thing you must do is get yourself into class," Deke said. He looked at his wristwatch. "Half of the eleven o'clock class is left. Get to it right now. Apologize to the teacher. Tell her you'll explain later. She'll accept that for now."

Deke sat in the reception room outside Wilfred Mulholland's office. The principal was on the telephone behind the closed door to his office, the secretary explained. A library matter, she said, involving a school-board member.

Deke was grateful for the delay. He needed a few moments to marshal his thoughts. He needed to frame his words in his mind. Things were moving past him in a whirlwind. The few moments alone were useful.

Deke's first move after Bobby left his office had been

to seek out Arnie Hamilton. The veteran football coach had worked with Wilfred Mulholland for twenty years. Arnie knew the principal as well as anyone.

Deke filled Arnie in on the developments of the morning and asked the question: "Will Mulholland back off his decison and give Bobby one more chance?"

Arnie frowned and patted his stomach and considered the question. "Mulholland is a tough cookie, and he figures that his job is to run the school and run it right," he said. "But you can be sure that he'll have the boy's interests at heart. You can be sure of it. I've never known Mulholland to be stubborn or inflexible. No, I'd say that you've got a chance with him, but it's never a lead-pipe cinch."

Arnie's words, which Deke considered to be encouraging, were moving through Deke's mind when the office door opened suddenly and Mulholland appeared. He was wearing his overcoat, obviously on his way to a luncheon appointment outside the school. Before his secretary could speak, he stopped in surprise at seeing Deke sitting in the reception room.

"Do you need to see me?" Mulholland asked. Then he added, without waiting for an answer, "Right now?"

Deke got to his feet. "If I may, for only a moment," he said. "It's very important."

Mulholland hesitated only a second. Then he turned to his secretary. "Please call the hotel dining room and leave word for Mr. Henderson that I will be a few minutes late," he said. Then to Deke, "Come in."

Mulholland took off his overcoat as he walked back into his office. He dropped the overcoat on a chair and gestured to another for Deke as he walked behind his desk. Deke seated himself across the desk from Mulholland.

As briefly as possible, Deke outlined the developments.

Mulholland listened without comment. His forehead wrinkled slightly when Deke related the details of Bobby's encounter with the police. But here, too, Mulholland remained silent, listening.

"What it all comes down to," Deke said, leaning forward, "is that we are facing a critical juncture—the last chance, I'm afraid—with this boy. He is finally willing to take the opportunity to join the team—join the group—and become a part of something that is good for him and important to him. And the other players are finally willing to extend themselves to help him do it." Deke paused. His voice was trembling slightly. He wished he could bring it under control. "We must give him this chance," he said. "It's important. Critical."

Mulholland tapped his desk lightly with his right forefinger. He said nothing for a moment. Then, more to himself than Deke, he said, "Discipline is based on consistency."

Deke's heart sank. On the face of it, Bobby did deserve punishment. Bobby had, in fact, cut classes, and not for the first time. His record, if that was all that mattered, did not warrant making an exception at this time. Did the fact he was a basketball player warrant making an exception? No, thought Deke, it does not. He was sure that Mulholland agreed. What about the next Bloomfield High student who compiles a similar record but is not a basketball player? Does he get off the hook? In a way, Bobby's preeminence as a basketball player was working against him at this moment.

Deke felt a horrible sense of failure. Arnie had indicated that Deke had every reason to hope for success, if he presented his case effectively. But now he was not finding success. He was finding failure. It was his own fault.

"You say that he is in class now, that he came in on his own initiative and returned to class?" Mulholland asked.

"That's right."

Mulholland continued to tap the desk lightly with his finger. The seconds seemed like hours to Deke. The light tapping on the desk sounded like drumbeats in the silence of the room.

"All right," Mulholland said suddenly. "Let's give it a try. Let's take the gamble. Let's give the lad his chance. I'll go along with you."

Deke nodded automatically. He was unable to believe his ears. Mulholland had seemed so obviously going in the other direction for his decision. Then Deke smiled. "You won't regret it, sir," he said. Deke was sure he was right.

Mulholland, standing up and reaching for his overcoat, grinned slightly at Deke. He said, "You forgot to mention how badly the Bulldogs need Bobby Haggard's outside shooting against Mount Perry."

"I—"

"I'm pleased that you did not mention it," Mulholland said.

20

By the time the players began drifting into the locker room to dress for practice, Deke was breathing easily. The morning had been a wild roller-coaster ride of ups and downs for Deke. He had started at the bottom, worrying about the tension left over from the freeze-out. He had soared with the word of the team's decision from Skipper and Benjy. He had plummeted listening to Wilfred Mulholland tell of Bobby's truancy. He started back up again during the visit with Bobby and reached the heights with Mulholland's final decision.

But even at noon, walking out of Mulholland's office with a smile on his face, Deke knew that two important tasks remained. Mishandled, either of them was capable of sending Deke's roller-coaster ride plunging again.

First, Deke sought out Skipper in the school cafeteria.

"You've heard?" Deke asked. He and Skipper were seated together at the end of a long table where Deke had led Skipper after pulling him out of the food line. "You know what's happened?"

Yes, Skipper knew. Everyone knew. The word was all over the school. Bobby's companions in the car the night before had spent the morning boasting about their adventure.

The expression on Skipper's face registered his disapproval. Deke was able to understand why Bobby called Skipper a snob. Skipper behaved himself, had no patience with those who didn't—and made no secret of either fact. That did not add up to snobbery, of course. But Deke was able to see why Bobby found it so difficult to extend himself to Skipper.

Deke leaned across the table, speaking softly, and related his conversation with Bobby and then the conversation with Mulholland.

Skipper listened without speaking. His expression offered no clue to what was going through his mind.

"Bobby was changing his ways when he came back to the team after the Warfield Tech game," Deke said. "You know it. You told me so. But you froze him out against Adamsville East last night."

Skipper shifted uncomfortably in his chair. "We told you this morning—"

"I know, I know," Deke said. "And I'm not saying,

not at all, that the freeze-out was in any way a valid excuse for the trouble Bobby got himself into after the game." Deke paused. "The point is, Bobby is ready to put all the problems and the troubles behind him now. The rest of you must do the same. We've got a chance now to get everything together. We must not lose that chance. It is important—to Bobby, to me, and to you and all the other players." Deke leaned back and waited.

Skipper was silent a moment. Then he asked, "What do you want me to do?"

"You know what I want you to do: make sure that everyone understands and agrees."

From the cafeteria, Deke returned to his office, closed the door, sat down at his desk, and dialed Herbie Foxx's telephone number at the station.

Deke had no doubt that Skipper would deliver on his end of the job. Skipper was not the snob that Bobby thought him to be, despite his manner. Skipper had proved that this morning. An honorable person, Skipper saw the wrong in the freeze-out. He would make up for it. As the leader of the team, Skipper would be able to sway any doubters.

Herbie Foxx came on the line. "I just heard that Bobby's not in school at all today," Herbie snapped. "You didn't tell me that."

Deke sighed. He had hoped to tell Herbie about Bobby's truancy himself at the same time he told him how the problem had been resolved. But Deke was not surprised Herbie had learned of it elsewhere. The veteran sportscaster had contacts all over Bloomfield. Undoubtedly, he had inquired about Bobby in the wake of the previous night's troubles. Somebody had told him that Bobby was absent and unaccounted for.

"I did not know all the facts when we spoke earlier," Deke said carefully. "I know the facts now. That's why I'm calling you. To tell you what's happened."

"Okay, shoot."

Deke repeated the events of the morning in detail. He left nothing out. He was taking a long-shot gamble, he knew, by bringing the broadcaster into his confidence. The story, broadcast on Herbie's evening radio show, would have a devastating effect on the team. But Herbie was bound to piece it together eventually. He was a digging reporter. If he got the story on his own, he surely would go on the air with it. But this way, getting the story in full from Deke, perhaps. . . .

Herbie waited until Deke had finished speaking. "So it looks like Bobby will be in there for the Mount Perry game, and that there won't be any more freeze-outs," he said.

"I think that is correct."

"You think?"

"Herbie, the way things have been going today I wouldn't bet that the sun will set in the west this evening," Deke said. "But, yes, I do think that everything is settled, and we're all together now at last."

Herbie chuckled slightly. There was a pause, and then he said, "I'm waiting for you to ask me not to use any of this on the air."

"I'm assuming that you won't, for the good of everyone involved, and particularly for the good of Bobby Haggard."

"Don't worry," Herbie said. Then he added, "Unless, of course, it doesn't work."

Deke held the telephone a moment without speaking. Yes, of course. Unless it doesn't work. Deke had not considered the possibility of failure. There had been no time for it. He felt like the juggler he had seen on television as a child. The juggler started with three balls. An assistant, off to the side, tossed another ball into the action every few moments. The juggler, feet spread, knees bent, head thrown back looking up at the balls, went faster and faster and faster. Finally, there came one ball too many. All the balls fell. Until that moment, the juggler had no time to think of failure. And until this moment Deke, through all the ups and downs of the last few hours, was racing with the events without time for considering failure.

"In that case," Herbie said, "I'll go on the air with the story. My responsibility is to my listeners. Clair Thornton might be here now, God forbid, if I hadn't told the town what was happening."

Deke let Herbie do the talking. Deke had what he had called for: the broadcaster's promise to keep the story to himself, at least for the present. Herbie's promise was the last piece in the puzzle. It was the final necessary ingredient needed to win the Bulldogs' struggle with "the Bobby Haggard problem." And Deke had the promise. So he let Herbie talk. Herbie's postscript to his promise didn't matter. Herbie was threatening to tell the story of the freeze-out, the truancy, Deke's inability to control the players and settle the team down, if things fell apart. But it didn't matter. If the delicate fabric unraveled,

Deke and Bobby and all the players were losers, no matter what Herbie Foxx said on the air. In that event, Herbie's comments could not make matters any worse. In fact, if the Bulldogs did pull themselves together, the story could be told later with no harm done. What mattered was the two days between now and the Mount Perry game, and Deke had Herbie's promise on that.

"If everything is straightened out and Bobby is in there, you ought to beat Mount Perry," Herbie announced.

"I hope you're right," Deke said.

As the players were changing their clothes, moving about the locker room picking up their gear, Deke was pulling on his sweat suit for the practice session.

The game plan for Mount Perry was completed, thanks to Deke's decision to skip lunch and work through the afternoon at his desk. Deke was satisfied with it. But the roller-coaster ride was not over.

"I've got something to say," Bobby announced suddenly.

Deke gulped and blinked.

The other players looked up, startled. They were motionless, their eyes on Bobby.

Bobby was standing in front of his locker, facing the room. He had finished dressing for practice. He stood there, staring at a blank space across the room. He looked very serious.

The room was quiet. Nobody said anything. Everyone was waiting.

Deke felt a churning sensation in his stomach. He

could not help fearing the worst. Now, with everything —*everything*—set so carefully in place, ready to mesh, what was happening? After a frantic day of trying to fit everything together, had Deke missed the most important move of all? He had not, in the rush of events, told Bobby: shut your mouth, and keep it shut. Deke wished he had.

Bobby, speaking a little too loudly in his nervousness, began describing the episode of the night before. In short, choppy sentences, he told everything. Some of the people in the car were drinking, the driver was speeding, the police found marijuana cigarettes in the car, they all spent a while at the police station.

"I want you to know what happened," Bobby said. "I want you to hear it from me." The tone of his voice made clear that he had more to say.

Deke made no move to cut Bobby off. The churning in his stomach had stopped. This looked and sounded like a different Bobby Haggard. Bobby had decided to change his ways after the Warfield Tech game. But he had not announced the fact, and some of the players had failed to notice then or failed to believe what they saw. This time Bobby was laying it out for them. Gone was the last trace of the cocky, defiant tone of voice, the slightest hint of the arrogant half grin. And gone, too, it seemed, was the compulsion to strike out at those around him, before they could strike out at him. Deke glanced at the players in the locker room. Their faces wore expressions of attention and interest—and, for the first time, sympathy and understanding. But maybe

Deke's imagination was getting the best of him. He waited for Bobby to continue.

"I let you down when I got myself suspended and missed the Warfield Tech game. I know it. And during those days that I was out, I did a lot of thinking. I came back on Monday determined to make it up to you—to make up for the stupidity, make up for the loss, make up for everything. I knew then how very much I want to be a member of this basketball team. But you froze me out."

Bobby glanced down at the floor, then looked back up. He smiled nervously. "Maybe I should have made this speech earlier," he said. And he added, almost parenthetically, "Maybe there are a lot of things I should have done before now."

Nobody said anything. Nobody changed expression.

"Or maybe one of you should have made this speech earlier," Bobby said.

For an instant, Deke thought he saw a trace of the old Bobby Haggard arrogance flash across his face. Around the room, the other players exchanged glances. Deke waited, his feeling of uneasiness returning.

"Let's lay it all out," Bobby said. "It's about time we did." He paused. "I did things that were wrong, and they hurt this team. You did, too—wrong things that hurt this team. But I—I'm not doing these things anymore. I'm going to be a good team member. If you will . . . ."

Deke understood the words sticking in Bobby's throat. The slender redhead was a tough kid. He did not request favors. And he granted none. This kind of talk was hard for him.

"What I'm trying to say is," Bobby continued, his voice barely above a whisper, "let's start over, let's get together, all of us, and play like a team, and we can beat those guys from Mount Perry on Friday night—and beat anybody else, too."

Bobby glanced quickly at Deke. He seemed embarrassed and uncertain what to do or say, now that he had concluded.

Deke nodded slightly to Bobby.

The silence remained in the room for a moment. Bobby began walking out of the locker room toward the court.

"Wait a minute," Skipper said.

Deke looked at Skipper. The senior forward was wearing his usual serious, almost stern expression.

Bobby turned in the doorway and faced Skipper.

Skipper suddenly grinned. "That's a good idea, beating Mount Perry on Friday night, and then beating everybody else."

"Let's go," Deke said, getting to his feet. "We've got a lot of work to do."

21

Deke Warden looked around the Bloomfield High gym and decided he never had seen anything like this at a high-school basketball game.

Hundreds of Bulldog basketball games had gone into the record books in this gymnasium. A lot of them had been important games. Significant or not, the gym always was filled to capacity. But Deke was sure that never before had there been such an overflow crowd jamming the bleachers and streaming through the doors as to-night.

Every few minutes the announcer issued an urgent plea over the loudspeaker: "All right now, let's everybody in the bleachers move in a little closer. Let's tighten it up so we can seat everybody."

At the far end of the court, student ushers were setting up folding chairs along the boundary lines of the playing court. They would accommodate some of the overflow crowd. And at the near end of the court, more folding chairs were stacked against the wall, to be set up in the aisles when the doors finally were closed.

Fire Chief Nicholas Kaufmann was much in evidence, directing the student ushers in their activities so that some sort of emergency exit aisles would be left. But it seemed the fire chief was more interested in arranging the chairs as tightly as possible than providing safety aisles. He was a leading Bulldog rooter.

Through the doors, Deke could see more people milling around in the lobby, hoping to get inside while a seat remained. Clearly, however, the gym would not be able to hold all of them.

Back under the bleachers, in its usual corner, the Bloomfield High combo blared out a fight song.

Many of the fans were from Mount Perry. Excited by the Tigers' undefeated season, they had been forming large automobile caravans for trips to the out-of-town games. They were certain that their team was headed for the state championship. The Tigers had barely missed last year. The Mount Perry fans were sure they would make it this year, and they did not want to miss a single minute of the historic season.

The Bloomfield fans were out in record numbers, too. Just the chance to see the Mount Perry Tigers in action was a strong drawing card for anyone loving basketball.

But more than that, the Bloomfield fans knew that their Bulldogs might knock off the high-riding Tigers. With the little redhead in there pumping them in from the outside, anything was possible.

The loss to Warfield Tech and the sluggish game against Adamsville East were behind them. Everybody in town knew the explanation for the loss to Warfield Tech. But Bobby was here tonight to face the Mount Perry Tigers. As for the Bulldogs' dull performance against Adamsville East, the fans seemed to accept Deke's simple explanation: "An off night." The fans also added another explanation of their own: "The boys were looking ahead to the Mount Perry game."

No one had talked of the freeze-out against Bobby in the Adamsville East game. Thanks to Herbie Foxx's cooperation, the subject never came up publicly. And the fans themselves, if they suspected a freeze-out, forgot about it. There was no freeze-out in the last three quarters, and the Bulldogs won.

All the signs pointed to an upset victory over Mount Perry for the Bulldogs, and a victory fever had swept through Bloomfield in the last two days. Herbie Foxx's nightly reports of the Bulldogs' good practice sessions fanned the flames. By game time, the fans had decided that the Bulldogs were going to defeat Mount Perry for sure.

On the court in front of Deke, the Bulldogs in their bright-green warm-up jackets were shooting a half-dozen basketballs toward the hoop.

To Deke, the Bulldogs looked ready to play their best. The concentration was evident on the faces of the players. Yet, their physical movements were loose, easy, relaxed.

Deke glanced to his right, where the Mount Perry Tigers were taking their warm-up shots. Deke recognized the individuals on the Mount Perry team. He had watched and rewatched the Mount Perry players in action on the videotape at the Peoria television station on Sunday afternon, and ever since he had seen them in his mind time and again as he worked over his notes. He saw them in their small failures and their successes as he carved out his game plan. He knew their every move.

At a glance, the Tigers seemed to have it all. They were a tall, strong team. They had speed in the right places. They had poise. They could shoot, dribble, and pass. The reasons for their 9–0 record showed in every play. It was no wonder they were rolling over every team they played.

No question, the size and talent of their personnel gave them a tremendous advantage over the Bulldogs.

But Deke had told himself time and again as he stared at the films and scoured his notes: Any basketball team can be defeated.

Now, as he watched the Tigers warming up, almost casual in their confidence, he wondered if the tiny flaws he had spotted would be enough. And he wondered if his Bulldogs would have the skill and determination to take advantage of the flaws.

Sherm Wallace, standing six feet, eight inches tall, was stuffing the ball in the basket, and some of the fans at that end of the court responded with soft calls of, "Ooooooh."

Wallace was two inches taller than Benjy Holman, and he was a good jumper. Deke had no doubts that Wallace could outjump Benjy. Wallace was a strong rebounder and a good shooter from under the basket.

But those three words, *under the basket*, revealed a weakness. Wallace was not an outstanding shooter from as far as fifteen feet out. So the Bloomfield defense would try to tie him up under the basket, knowing that if he moved out, he presented less of a scoring threat.

As a defensive player, Wallace was awesome on the backboards. But here, too, the three words, *under the basket*, were important. The Bulldogs would try to pull him out from under the basket. Benjy would play a high post, operating near the top of the free-throw circle. Benjy could score from that distance. His hook shots were the only chance against the taller, stronger Wallace.

Deke had spotted another clue related to the three little words, *under the basket*. Wallace tended to get rough and foul, trying to get back in under the basket for a rebound. So there was a fringe benefit in luring the big Mount Perry center out from under the basket. Maybe he would foul out.

Deke learned a secret about the Mount Perry guards, too. Robbie Ashford and George Kane almost qualified as twins. They looked alike, and they played alike. Each stood an even six feet in height. They were thin but muscular, not skinny. They were strong and quick. Both were capable of ducking a shoulder and dribbling through for a lay-up at any moment. Both were outstanding with the long shots. But it was there, in the shots from the outside, that Deke found a weakness. Again, they were alike. Both had the weakness. Deke noticed that they scored with greater consistency from the outside when they were being harassed by a defender. When shooting quickly, they hit the basket. Relying solely on instinct and basic shooting ability developed through hours of practice, they scored on a high percentage of their shots. But when they took their time, the shots more often were off the mark. Given a split second to think about it, they frequently missed. Deke had seen it before. In fact, he had had a bit of the same trouble himself in his playing days.

The forwards, Billy Altheimer and Paul Crowe, were sure to be problems. They were deadeye shots from the corners, strong rebounders, good dribblers who could go inside for lay-up shots. If they had weaknesses, Deke did not find them in the films.

Whether the Bulldogs could turn the Tigers' few weaknesses to their own advantage remained for the game to tell. More than Deke's game plan was required. The Bulldogs needed good shooting, good play execution, good defensive coordination, and, yes, good luck.

Deke took his eyes off the Tigers and turned when a group of the Bloomfield fans, up high on one of the top rows in the bleachers behind him, began the singsong chant: "Go-Bobby-Go! Go-Bobby-Go!"

When Deke turned back to the court, Skipper Denham was the one who was acknowledging the cheer with clenched fists upraised, a smile on his face. As for

Bobby, he was pumping a jump shot through the basket.

The warning buzzer sounded. The opening was seconds away.

Deke stepped forward to meet the players moving toward the bench.

22

The referee was standing in the center circle, holding the basketball loosely on his hip, awaiting the players for the game's tip-off. The arc lights from the ceiling bathed the scene. The referee, alone in the middle of the playing court, cast no shadow. Around him, the polished floor gleamed.

On all four sides of the court, in the bleachers and on the folding chairs, all the seats were taken. The doors to the lobby were closed now. The more fortunate of the late arrivals found standing room near the doors. At least they were inside. Others, unable to squeeze in, were still milling around in the lobby. If they stayed, they would be able to follow the progress of the game by listening to the announcements over the loudspeaker.

Despite the jam-packed crowd, the gym was strangely silent in those final seconds before the beginning of the game. There was an electricity in the air. Even the people in the bloc of seats reserved for Mount Perry fans were sitting quietly, staring intently at the scene before them.

At the Bloomfield bench, Deke Warden leaned into the circle of his players standing around him. All clasped hands in the center. They pumped once in unison. Then they broke the circle. The five starters turned to walk onto the court. Deke and the substitutes watched.

Deke had said nothing in the circle. Nothing was left to say in the last second. Everything had been said in the last three days. Now all that remained was to play the game. Only the game would tell whether the Bulldogs, in a little more than two days of feeling like a team, could reach full potential. The answer was in the action on the playing court, not in any last-second exhortation by the coach.

Deke stepped back and sat down on the bench. The substitutes also sat down. All of them, coach and players alike, as if striking some pose they had rehearsed, sat forward, elbows on knees, hands clasped in front of them, watching.

Already the Mount Perry Tigers were on the court. Deke noticed with a twinge that the Tigers exuded confidence. They walked like champions. They stood like champions. Their facial expressions did not change as they sized up the Bloomfield Bulldogs joining them on the court.

Deke heard again the confident words of Bernard MacKay. "We're not planning to lose again for a while."

The players were sorting each other out, getting themselves in position for the opening jump.

Deke thought he could read traces of casualness bordering on contempt in the expression of the Mount Perry players. He hoped so. Surprise was a part of his game plan, especially in the important first quarter. The Tigers had a record of running away with the game in the first quarter, galloping out to a 10–2 or 12–4 lead. The opponents never caught up. If the Bulldogs were, as Deke believed, ready to play their best game of the season, a little overconfidence in the Tigers at the outset was a valuable aid. The immediate problem was to keep the Tigers from charging into a commanding lead in the first few minutes.

The referee flipped the ball into the air and stepped back.

Benjy Holman and the taller, stronger Sherm Wallace went up for the ball. Wallace won.

Benjy had outjumped players two inches taller before. But he wasn't outjumping Sherm Wallace. The Mount Perry center was a good jumper.

Wallace tipped the ball to his right, into the waiting hands of Robbie Ashford, a guard. Without dribbling even once, Ashford fired a pass across the court to the other guard, George Kane, and the Tigers began moving toward the goal.

As the play unfolded, the quickness of the Tigers' action left Deke blinking. Kane hardly had taken in the pass from Ashford before he rifled the ball off to Billy Altheimer in a corner. Altheimer faked a jump shot, leaving Skipper flat-footed, and sent a one-handed pass back to Kane. Kane bounced the ball in to Wallace, now under the basket, and the big center went up and dumped the ball through the basket.

The scoreboard flickered: Bulldogs 0, Visitors 2.

The Mount Perry fans, seated together at one end of the bleachers, erupted in a standing cheer. This was what they had come to see.

For the Bloomfield fans, the play came as a shock. The quickness and power of the Tigers, going almost straight from the tip-off to a field goal, was not lost on the Bulldog rooters. They exchanged glances and shrugged.

The Tigers, moving into their defensive alignment, backpedaled past Deke's position on the bench. He was struck by their matter-of-fact attitude. They had just zipped in for a quick score on the opening play of the game. They were out front, and it had been easy. But there were no smiles. There were no shouts or cheers from the players. Just workmanlike expressions. All in a day's work.

Ken Flaherty tossed the ball inbounds to Bobby, and Bobby dribbled leisurely toward mid-court, watching the Mount Perry defenders set themselves for the attack.

At the center stripe, Bobby passed the ball back to Ken. Then Bobby cut across the court, toward the corner. The Mount Perry zone defense shifted slightly to accommodate the thrust. In the split second of opening during the shift, Ken fired a pass to Benjy under the basket. Bobby, racing in from the corner, came in behind Benjy. Wallace, taller and stronger, was smothering Benjy. Suddenly Benjy pivoted and handed off to Bobby running by under the basket. Bobby was clear, with Benjy screening off Wallace. Bobby dribbled once going under and flipped the ball up. The ball hit the backboard and fell through for a field goal.

Bobby was smiling as he curled out toward the center of the court, looking back in time to see the lay-up drop through. He kept going, moving to take up his defensive position.

On the bench, Deke exhaled. Benjy was smiling, too, knowing that the play had bypassed and outsmarted the highly touted Sherm Wallace.

But for the Bulldogs now the job was defense—stopping, somehow, the quick and sure hands of the guards, the sharpshooting of the forwards from the corners, and the jumping of Sherm Wallace.

Deke gestured slightly at Skipper passing by.

Skipper shouted, "Two!" It was the signal to pull the defense back into a tighter net, closer to the basket, as they had practiced.

Deke watched as the players tightened the zone, trying to bottle Wallace up sufficiently to render him helpless or force him to move out, where his shooting strength was reduced.

There were dangers. The guards would have more space and time for their operations on the edge of the zone. If they were left free and they pumped in a series of long shots, the result would be disaster. If the Tigers still were able to get the ball through to Wallace, the result would be disaster. It would mean that Wallace was unstoppable. If Wallace moved out and was able to score consistently, it would mean disaster.

Deke thought that the word *disaster* was popping up in his mind entirely too often. "Well," he said to himself, "we'll see."

23

By the end of the first quarter, Deke Warden was able to take a deep breath.

The scoreboard showed: Bulldogs 12, Visitors 14.

The Mount Perry Tigers had not run away with the game in the opening minutes. The two teams had traded points in the first eight minutes. Granted, Mount Perry never trailed. But, by the same token, the Tigers never enjoyed more than a three-point lead over the Bulldogs. Each time the Tigers appeared on the verge of pulling away, the Bulldogs came up with a field goal. The Bulldogs were, so far, keeping the Tigers from breaking open the game.

The score left an important part of Deke's game plan intact: hang in there and stay close; don't fall so far behind that there is no catching up; keep within striking distance. That way, and only that way, was there a chance of a late burst, winning the game for Bloomfield. The game could be won in the last two minutes. Deke was sure of it. But only if the Bulldogs were, miraculously, out front or, at worst, only a few points behind in the closing minutes.

Deke stood to greet the players approaching the bench for the brief intermission between quarters.

Benjy Holman, usually blank-faced, was smiling at something Skipper Denham was saying. Benjy had been the heavy artillery of the Bulldogs' attack in the first quarter. Three hook shots over the desperate lunges of Sherm Wallace had scored six points. He added one on a free throw when Wallace fouled him.

Four of the Bulldogs' other five points in the first period came from Bobby Haggard. First, Bobby zipped through in the opening minute for the lay-up shot behind Benjy's screening of Wallace. Later Bobby pumped in a twenty-five foot jump shot.

For Bobby, a score of four points in the first quarter was below the expectable. But Bobby's sharp passing was what put the ball in Benjy's hands for the hook shots that were keeping the Bulldogs in the running.

On defense, the tightening of the net around Wallace was paying off. At first, the Tigers ignored the Bulldogs' jamming of the passing route. They tried to fire the ball through the crowd to the big center. Then they gave up the tactic. The guards, in relative freedom, began firing away from the outside. They were hoping for points, of course. But even more, they wanted to lure the Bloomfield defense out and away from Wallace. Their shots scored often enough to concern Deke. The guards got eight of the Tigers' fourteen points in the first period. But Deke stuck to the close-in defense. The guards were missing more of their shots than they should, as Deke had figured.

As the Bulldogs approached Deke at the bench, he glanced once more at the scoreboard. His Bulldogs were down two points. For now, he considered the scoreboard's reading to be a triumph. But later, he knew, being down just one point spelled defeat.

Behind Deke, and all around the court, the Bloomfield fans clearly viewed the score as a victory for this stage of the game. The fans were on their feet with a roar when the buzzer ended the first quarter. They still were shouting. Somewhere in the noise, the rhythmic chant was coming through: "Go-Bobby-Go! Go-Bobby-Go!" The Bloomfield fans wanted to see the slender redhead standing at the edge of the keyhole and pumping in field goals. Deke did, too.

Deke pulled the players in close and shouted to make himself heard above the din.

To Benjy: "Stay on the high post. Keep hooking them over Wallace. He can't stop you. He's awkward trying to get back under the basket. He fouled you once. He'll do it again."

To Skipper and to Dennis North: "Stay on those forwards when they go to the corners. Both of them,

Altheimer and Crowe, are good. But you've held them scoreless so far. It's beautiful. Keep it up."

To Bobby and to Ken Flaherty: "Be alert for the full-court press. The Tigers can move their zone down the court after you. They love to do it. Be ready."

And to Bobby alone: "Start shooting from the outside more often."

The players were toweling off the perspiration. Each, in turn, nodded his understanding of Deke's shouted instructions. The intermission was ending. They clasped hands, the five players and the coach, and pumped once in unison.

Deke held their hands in the clasp for a moment. Turning his head around the group, he shouted above the roar of the crowd: "We're right on schedule. . . . Perfect. . . . Just keep going."

The deafening shouts of the crowd increased as the players returned to the court. The cheerleaders scampered off the court, going back to their places at the courtside.

Again Wallace outjumped Benjy on the tip-off. The big Mount Perry center deftly flicked the ball over to the guard, Robbie Ashford, who zipped a quick pass to George Kane. Kane dribbled a moment in place, sizing up the scene before him. Then, with both hands, he sent a high pass toward Wallace under the basket.

Wallace got the ball. He came down, dribbled once, and started back up. Benjy was with him, but not high enough. Skipper moved in for the rebound in case Wallace's shot missed the mark. But Wallace did not shoot for the basket. He turned and dropped off a pass to Crowe at the forward's position in the corner.

Skipper, too late, slammed on the brakes and turned to cover the vacant area he had left behind.

Crowe, alone for a second, shot and hit. The Tigers' lead widened to 16–12.

On the bench, Deke remained almost motionless in the pose he had held through the first quarter. Hunched forward, elbows on knees, hands gripped tightly together in front of him, Deke stared intently at the action. Only his head moved.

For Deke, the first quarter had passed in a series of pictures appearing before his eyes. Each shot, each pass, each movement of the ball was a picture. The pictures flickered by like the frames of a movie in slow motion. This second quarter was the same. The first picture, Skipper frantically trying to reverse himself while Crowe set himself for the shot, was a bad one. It had cost the Bulldogs a field goal.

Ken flipped the ball inbounds to Bobby to resume the play following the Mount Perry field goal. There was no sign of the Tigers' celebrated full-court zone defense, copied from the halcyon days of UCLA's basketball power. Deke was a little surprised.

Bobby dribbled up the court. At the center stripe, he passed back to Ken, who sent a quick pass back to Bobby. Benjy was roving in and out of the corridor in front of the basket, out around the free-throw line. Wallace was looming behind Benjy.

Bobby shot a pass toward Benjy.

Out of nowhere, Ashford flashed into view and took

a stab at the ball. He got only a piece of the ball. But it was enough. The pass, deflected, bounced off Benjy's outstretched fingers. Wallace, coming forward, reached for the ball at the same instant Benjy was turning to try for a recovery. The ball squirted away from the two of them and into the hands of the Mount Perry forward, Altheimer.

Altheimer straightened with the ball in his hands and looked downcourt. Already Crowe was there, racing toward the basket, a hand held high. Altheimer uncorked a baseball pass. Crowe took it on the run, dribbled once, and laid it up.

Bobby and Ken both were there an instant later. But it was exactly that—an instant late. The ball dropped through the net for two points.

Now the difference was six points, 18–12. And Deke had another bad picture in the long sequence of scenes being etched in his mind.

From there, the second quarter was a replay of the first quarter, with the two teams trading points. By the luck of the clock, the Bulldogs got the last field goal in the long series of trades and went into the half-time intermission trailing by four points, 32–28. Again Benjy's hook shots from outside the hovering Wallace, and Bobby's scoring ability from the outside had enabled the Bulldogs to cling to a chance. Benjy hooked in three field goals. Bobby got three and a free throw.

But, Deke thought, as he walked toward the dressing room for the half-time intermission, close does not win. The time for trading points has got to end.

24

Deke Warden let most of the half-time intermission in the dressing room go for rest and relaxation. He had but two points to make.

"First," he told the Bulldogs, "let's look at one play. Just one play. It's very revealing."

The players, slumped on the benches toweling themselves, watched Deke as he spoke.

"Very early in the second quarter, when we were four points behind, we were bringing the ball up the court after a Mount Perry field goal," Deke recounted. "Instead of scoring, we lost the ball. A turnover. I'm not assessing the blame. I don't even know if anybody is to blame. The Tigers made the turnover happen. But that's not my point. The turnover cost us four points—not two points, but four points. Instead of scoring two points ourselves, we let the Tigers take the ball away and score two points for themselves. Two less for us, two more for them, four points in the difference. If that one play—one play!—had not gone the way it did, we would be tied with Mount Perry right now, instead of trailing by four points."

Deke looked around at the players. None of them said anything.

"Tomorrow, when you're thinking back over this game, and we've won or we've lost," Deke said, "you're going to be able to pinpoint certain plays—certain moments in the game—that made all the difference in the end."

Deke decided against belaboring the point that every single play was important. If the players did not understand now, nothing he said mattered.

"Second, and this is an obvious point," Deke said. "We have to outscore Mount Perry in the second half. The time has passed for hanging in there and staying close. You've done the job so far. But there's a different job ahead of us now."

Deke pointed at Bobby Haggard. "Like they say, 'Go-Bobby-Go!' " Deke said softly. "The time has come to put points on the board and go into the lead. Bobby, you keep pumping for the basket from the outside. And Benjy, you keep Wallace out from under the basket.

And Skipper and Ken and Dennis, you be ready. If Bobby hits, the rest of you will be finding yourselves open."

He was putting the pressure squarely on the little redhead, Deke knew. But with or without Deke's words, the pressure was on Bobby. He was the outside shooter the Bulldogs had needed from the first day of the season. Now was the time to collect on his talents. Deke knew it, Bobby knew it, and so did everybody else in the room. There had been trouble and dissension, sure, but the team members had acknowledged they needed Bobby Haggard, and Bobby knew that he needed the team. There was no reason, Deke felt, to leave anything unsaid at this point.

Bobby, his face serious, draped a towel loosely around his neck and watched Deke without answering.

Back on the court, with his Bulldogs taking their warm-up shots, Deke noticed with some satisfaction that the Mount Perry Tigers were wearing different expressions on their faces. Not that the look of confidence was gone. It was still there. The Tigers had won too many games not to figure they could win one more. But gone was the expression of arrogance, the look of contempt. They were taking nothing for granted now. A shadow of worry showed in their faces.

The four points of difference in the score, while seeming to Deke and his Bulldogs to be an enormous gap to overcome, was closer than the Tigers expected or liked. They knew they had a difficult second half in front of them. Bloomfield was hanging in there. The Bulldogs were keeping pace. The passes to Sherm Wallace were not getting through with the usual regularity. The Bloomfield defense was refusing to be lured out by the long shots of the guards. The Bulldogs' little redhead was hard to stop. If he got hot, the four-point lead would evaporate before their eyes. And the big center was deadly with his hook shots. Wallace seemed powerless to stop him.

Deke understood the Tigers' feelings as he looked them over lining up for the start of the second half.

The gym was all noise and lights as the Bulldogs moved out to join the Tigers for the tip-off. The Bloomfield fans were on their feet, as they had been during most of the first half. The Bloomfield High combo was allowing the last blaring sounds of a fight song to fade out. The Mount Perry fans, bunched together in the far bleachers, let out a cheer for their team. But they were a serious-looking group.

As for Bernard MacKay, the Mount Perry coach, he was standing on the boundary stripe, hands on hips, shouting something that nobody on the court could hear. One of the Mount Perry guards, Robbie Ashford, was cupping a hand to his ear to signal the coach that he was not receiving the message.

Deke sat down on the bench. He leaned forward and watched.

The referee tossed the ball into the air. Wallace outjumped Benjy again. But Bobby raced out of his position and speared the ball with an outstretched hand before it reached George Kane, the guard Wallace was aiming for.

The loose ball bounced into Skipper's hands. Skipper

dribbled toward the sideline and flipped a pass to Bobby. Bobby dribbled twice, stopped, and fired a quick set shot toward the basket. The arching course of the ball covered at least twenty-five feet. Seeming to float, the ball went up, up and then down, down and—swoosh!

Bobby grinned as he turned and headed back up the court. Skipper shot both fists into the air. His smile was wider than Bobby's.

Deke knew the thought that was flashing through all their minds: a four-point play. Instead of letting Mount Perry take the winning tip-off and move in for a field goal, they had stolen the ball and put it through for two points for themselves.

Bobby, with four points in the first quarter and seven in the second quarter, now had thirteen points.

The scoreboard flickered: Bulldogs 30, Visitors 32. On the Mount Perry bench, MacKay signaled for a time-out.

At first, the Mount Perry coach's tactics surprised and puzzled Deke. But then he knew what was in MacKay's mind. First, he wanted to give his players a moment's respite to recover from the sudden turn of events, pulling the Bulldogs within two points. And second, he wanted to make sure everyone understood that Bobby's swishing long shot was not a fluke. The little redhead needed close watching.

Deke leaned into the circle of his players at the bench. "They were laying back, not expecting the long one," he said. "It won't happen next time. Be on your toes, and"—he looked at Bobby—"if they come out after you in force, look for Benjy or for Skipper and Dennis."

Deke was having to shout in an effort to be heard above the roar of the crowd. He wondered who, if anyone, heard him. But Bobby nodded in acknowledgment.

Deke looked Bobby in the eye for a moment. Bobby seemed nervous. He was feeling the pressure, no doubt. The success or failure of the Bulldogs' big push for the lead rode on Bobby's shots from the outside. For the Bulldogs' strategy to work, Bobby had to score. The points themselves were valuable, to be sure. But, also, the threat of points from Bobby's long shots would free Benjy and Skipper and Dennis. Bobby's performance in the next few minutes was critical for the Bulldogs.

"Everybody okay?" Deke asked finally.

The players nodded and returned to the court.

Bringing the ball down the court, the Tigers seemed more deliberate than before. Perhaps there was a better word: cautious. Either way, the time-out clearly had served the purpose of settling them down.

The guards moved the ball across the center stripe and settled into a passing pattern. Sherm Wallace moved under the basket. The forwards took up their positions on either side of the center.

Benjy followed Wallace like a shadow in front of the basket. The remainder of the Bloomfield zone defense shifted with every pass of the ball.

Then, in a beautifully orchestrated movement, the Tigers weaved themselves toward the near side of the court. It was a lopsided lineup. The Bloomfield zone shifted to meet the weight of the attack. Wallace remained under the basket. Then Kane zipped a pass to the forward, Crowe, in the corner. Dennis moved out against him.

Deke, seeing what was happening, instinctively said, "No."

But even if he had spoken loudly enough for Dennis to hear, it was too late. The play was working. There was no stopping it now.

With Dennis lured out, Wallace simply turned his back on Benjy and stood his ground. The split-second screen was enough. The corridor under the basket was open. Kane, having passed to Crowe, raced under the basket, took a return pass from Crowe, and laid it up for a field goal.

It was the same maneuver the Bulldogs themselves had used in the first quarter with Bobby dancing past a screen set up by Benjy.

On the bench, Deke, sitting forward with his elbows on his knees, turned his head and glanced at the scoreboard. Bulldogs 30, Visitors 34.

Deke turned back to the court, where Bobby was taking the pass inbounds from Ken to resume the play.

25

Deke Warden was no longer seated on the bench. He was standing at the boundary line.

All around him, the hundreds of fans were on their feet shouting. The noise rolled down out of the bleachers in one unending wave.

Deke looked at the clock: one minute and thirty-two seconds remaining in the game. He looked at the scoreboard. He already knew the figures that were there: Bulldogs 54, Visitors 53.

Bobby's jump shot from the edge of the keyhole had swished through the nets, putting the Bulldogs out front for the first time in the game.

The gym was in pandemonium. The throbbing chant rocked the gym: "Go-Bobby-Go! Go-Bobby-Go!" The slender redhead had plunked in four in a row from more than twenty feet out.

Desperately the Mount Perry Tigers were swarming around him. But still, from the midst of the crowd, Bobby was getting the shots off.

Now, having put the Bulldogs out front, Bobby turned and moved up the court to take his defensive position. He was not smiling; he was dead serious. He and everyone else knew that the field goal was worthless if the Bulldogs were unable to stop the Tigers' assault.

Even in the face of crisis, the Tigers maintained their composure. Ashford, dribbling the ball toward the center stripe, glanced back over his shoulder at the clock. The seconds were ticking off. The clock showed: one minute and twenty-two seconds remaining. Plenty of time for Mount Perry. Plenty of time. The Tigers knew it. So did Deke.

The Bulldogs were backpedaling in front of the advancing Mount Perry Tigers. Deke, in his excitement, was waving an arm, urging his Bulldogs to hurry into their positions in the zone defense.

The huge Sherm Wallace took up his position under the basket. He was carrying four fouls now. One more would put him on the bench. He was on thin ice for the last minute and a half of the game. He knew it. His caution showed as he maneuvered around Benjy Holman, moving in and out of the corridor in front of the basket.

Ashford dribbled across the center stripe and passed

to his fellow guard, Kane. Kane dribbled once and, suddenly, sent a high pass toward Wallace under the basket. The ball soared over Benjy's outstretched hands. The sure fingers of Wallace grabbed the ball and hung on. Wallace turned and laid the ball on the rim. The ball sat there for what seemed to be a full minute. Then it rolled gently on the rim a few inches—and fell off.

Benjy was up, grabbing for the ball. So was Wallace. The two large boys came down with a crash. The ball was somewhere between them.

A jump ball resulting from both players having a share of possession would be bad news for the Bulldogs. Wallace was outjumping Benjy every time. And he would again.

Out of the tangle, Benjy jerked with everything he had and pivoted. He had the ball.

Wallace, stronger and just as quick as Benjy, had lost. The reason, surely, was the bit of timidity, the extra caution, that comes with having four fouls. One more means out of the game. Wallace was being careful. Benjy, who wasn't, took the ball away from him. Wallace's tendency to foul coming in under the basket was hurting the Tigers, even if he did not foul out of the game.

The clock was ticking down. Less than a minute remained. Forty-eight seconds.

Benjy was twisting and wriggling, continuing to pivot on his right foot, holding the ball in close, against the reaching hands of frantic Mount Perry guards.

The referee's whistle stopped the play. The Mount Perry forward Altheimer, dejectedly lifted a hand for the scorekeeper to see. Altheimer, slapping at the ball, had fouled Benjy.

At this stage, it was a one-and-one: If Benjy made the first free throw, he was entitled to a second.

Changing ends of the court, the teams lined up. Benjy took a deep breath and exhaled. He straightened up. He fired. His one-handed push shot arched toward the basket. It dropped through.

The scoreboard changed: Bulldogs 55, Visitors 53. The crowd roared, then fell silent for Benjy's second shot.

Benjy took another deep breath and pumped his one-handed push shot toward the basket. It dropped through. Bulldogs 56, Visitors 53.

Deke stared at the scoreboard. More than a field goal's difference now. Only forty seconds remaining. Barring a Mount Perry miracle, the Bulldogs were the winners.

The two Mount Perry guards, Ashford and Kane, exchanged the ball coming up the court. There was nothing casual about their approach this time. They were in a hurry. The Tigers needed two field goals to win. And the clock was ticking away. Thirty-five seconds remaining.

Kane crossed the center stripe and fired a pass along the boundary line to the forward, Altheimer, in the corner. The ball never got there.

Bobby lunged to the side and got both hands on the pass. Turning quickly to stay inbounds, he fell, hugging the ball to his stomach. Altheimer came out of the corner and got his hands on the ball.

The referee called for a jump. Twenty-eight seconds remaining.

Altheimer, at six feet, four inches tall, would easily outjump Bobby, at five feet, seven inches. The jump was taking place just a few yards from the basket where the Mount Perry Tigers needed to put the ball for a field goal.

Altheimer tipped the ball to Crowe, who leaped into the air and turned and shot—swish!

The scoreboard showed: Bulldogs 56, Visitors 55. Twenty-five seconds remaining.

Bulldogs' ball to bring inbounds. The Mount Perry full-court zone press, so long in coming, appeared now.

Ken Flaherty managed to get the ball inbounds to Bobby. But the Mount Perry defenders were swarming all over the end of the court, determined to steal the ball or, at least, prevent the Bulldogs from advancing over the center stripe within the prescribed ten seconds. That would give them possession, with time for a game-winning shot.

Bobby, dribbling low, headed for mid-court. Running into a wall of waving hands, he doubled back and dribbled across court.

Nineteen seconds remaining in the game. Four seconds remaining for the Bulldogs to cross the center stripe.

Bobby stopped. He sent a bounce pass toward the center stripe. Skipper, at the line, got it. Bobby raced across the center stripe. Skipper passed back to Bobby. The Mount Perry defenders converged on the small form, bent low, dribbling in circles.

The crowd was counting down the seconds: Fourteen . . . thirteen . . . twelve. . . .

Bobby weaved in and out of the Mount Perry players.

Six . . . five . . . four . . . three . . . two . . . one. . . .

The buzzer ended the game The fans swept down out of the bleachers and covered the playing court.

Deke rushed onto the court through the crowd and grabbed the first of his players that he encountered, Benjy, in a bear hug.

Past Benjy, Deke caught a glimpse of Bobby, a wide smile on his face, still holding the ball, just before the slender redhead disappeared in the surrounding crowd.

Finally, with the dressing room cleared of everyone except the team, Deke held both hands high in the air for attention.

The players looked at him.

"You were beautiful," Deke said. "You were perfect."

The players answered him with a loud cheer.

Deke looked around at their smiling faces. They were entitled to cheer themselves. They earned the right.

Benjy, seated on a bench, was clearly worn to a frazzle. He had played the entire game without a minute's relief. Thirty-two solid minutes of battling Sherm Wallace, the best high-school center in the state. Best until now, that is. Benjy had whipped Sherm Wallace. The smile on Benjy's face showed that he knew it.

Chris was laughing about something and pointing at Dennis North. Chris's smile was in sharp contrast to the expression he had worn stepping out of the van just three nights before. Chris was the only substitute who played.

Benjy and Bobby had played the entire game, all thirty-two minutes. But Chris had logged court time spelling Skipper and Ken and Dennis for brief rests. He was a part of the victory, and he was enjoying it.

Ken giggled in a silly way. He, more than any of the others, was revealing the enormous feeling of relief that comes when the pressure is suddenly lifted. Deke knew the feeling.

Skipper stood next to Benjy. He was still breathing heavily. But he was smiling as he wiped the perspiration off his forehead with a towel.

Even the substitutes who had seen no more action than the warm-up drills were shouting and cheering. For them, too, sitting on the bench, the game had been a long succession of tense moments. They, too, were winners of the big one.

Deke glanced at Bobby, whose wide smile revealed nothing of the long tortuous road that had brought him and the Bulldogs to this point. But, Deke reflected, his own smile at this moment probably showed none of the troubles plaguing the Bulldogs in the opening weeks of the season.

Deke waved his hands again for silence. "And—"

Bobby stepped into the center of the floor and interrupted Deke. He was wearing an impish grin. Or was it the cocky grin? "Let me tell you how I did it—"

Deke blinked and started to say something. Somebody sent a wet towel flying into Bobby's face. Everybody laughed.

When the towel fell to the floor, Bobby was laughing, too.

ABOUT THE AUTHOR

Thomas J. Dygard has been praised by *Booklist* as being "consistently one of the ablest writers of teenage sports fiction." He began his career as a sportswriter for the *Arkansas Gazette* in Little Rock and joined the Associated Press in 1954. In the years that followed, he worked in AP offices in Little Rock, Detroit, Birmingham, New Orleans, Indianapolis, Chicago, and Tokyo.

His popular books for young readers include *Halfback Tough, Outside Shooter, Quarterback Walk-on,* and *Tournament Upstart.*